The 3 Serpents of the North Door

D0993865

Serpent Books

Meeting House Hill | Norfolk

The 3 Serpents
of the North Door

By Saul Penfold

With illustrations by Jim Kavanagh
and a foreword by Emma Bridgewater

First published in Great Britain by Serpent Books, 2008
For more information, see www.serpentbooks.co.uk or write to us at
Cantelo Cottage, Meeting House Hill, Norfolk, NR28 9LR

ISBN 978-0-9558991-0-2
British Library Cataloguing in Publication Data
A catalogue record for this book is available from the British Library

Printed and bound by Postprint, Taverner House, Harling Road,
East Harling, Norfolk , NR16 2QR

Typeset and cover design by Paul Slack,
www.jamtartsandcustard.co.uk

Supported by

NORWICH
12
A journey through the English city

'The 3 Serpents of the North Door' is the first book in the
'City of Light' series

Acknowledgements

I am deeply grateful to the friends and colleagues who have helped with the development of this book. Many thanks to the Cathedral Friends Publishing Sub-Committee for its initial support and encouragement way back in the mists of time. In particular, to Elspeth MacKinlay for her editing and comments upon the first draft of the text and to Peter Siddons, for his expert final proof reading. I also owe much gratitude to the late John Nicholls for his friendship, inspiration and unfaltering enthusiasm.

There have been several drafts of this book and I would like to thank all those who have made insightful comments as the story has developed, in particular Maggie Cawkwell and Beryl Appleby.

This book would of course not be complete without the wonderful illustrations provided by Jim Kavanagh. For those, and for your ideas and good humour Jim, many thanks indeed — well done for hanging in there!

I am very grateful to Emma Bridgewater for her support and enthusiasm in writing the foreword and to Paul Slack for the wonderful cover design.

I would especially like to thank the many thousands of children and young people who visit Norwich Cathedral each year, bringing imagination, creativity and above all life to its ancient stones.

Lastly, to my wife Anne and to our two beautiful boys, with love.

For Alfie and Joseph, who bring magic

Foreword

Cathedrals are extraordinary places; extraordinarily big, old, full and mysterious. Visitors from all cultures are differently affected by these buildings, some by the Christian symbolism, some by the history and others by their spirituality. The fact that most of our cathedrals are in the middle of busy cities means that stepping from the frantic shopping street, dodging cars and buses into the quiet stillness of a medieval building involves something very close to time travel for all of us. Norwich Cathedral sits now in its Close, a visual reminder of its original context as part of a monastic complex. The Gatehouse, Refectory, Chapterhouse, Dormitory, Prior's Hall, Kitchens and Cloister all once surrounded the Cathedral itself. Each building had its own evolved purpose and between these, monks went about their daily round of work and prayer.

Today's Close is full of office workers eating sandwiches, commuters walking home, schoolboys going about their business and tramps about theirs. While their immediate concerns are of the present day, perhaps they are not completely un-affected by the medieval surroundings. Entering the Cathedral itself, even the most hardened atheist must pause. The soaring Nave supported by its massive stone Norman pillars with bold zigzag patterns or refined gothic clusters of beautifully carved shafts. Vaulted ceilings of unimaginable complexity and in the aisles, carvings of smiling skeletons and austere sleeping bishops, their elegant gaze hounds lying with them or on guard. Brasses in the floor commemorating long dead wimpled ladies and their helmeted warlike husbands are drawn with such immediacy that despite the stylized line it is easy to imagine that couple alive and walking through the church.

The Cathedral is a place where imagination runs riot, perhaps the only place in the modern city where signage, graphics, advertisements and musack have no place. Shorn of all these omnipresent stimuli a child is left on his or her own with the past and most importantly, with the power of the past. In these conditions snakes that coil coldly in limestone around a doorway can all too easily slither to the floor, gargoyles that have grimaced from a parapet for six hundred years can spit out their lead tube and whisper some violent threat and the retreating figure of a verger off to make a mug of tea and check his lottery ticket can become a self important fifteenth century monk off to check on the carp ponds. Perhaps children find this willing suspension of disbelief easier to achieve than adults, although half an hours immersion in the quiet of a church can often wipe out more everyday concerns than any other means.

Saul Penfold sees through the eyes of his youthful heroes, Tom and Emma Buxton, the hugely eventful and often very violent history of Norwich Cathedral. It is a story of brave knights and rude monks. It is a tantalizing view of the building of the church under the direction of Herbert de Losinga, the first Bishop, who's

Cathedral this was, the flaming riots of the thirteenth century, the destructive Civil War and Salvin's nineteenth century restoration of the building. But this is no guide book or dry history. The 3 Serpents is a gripping adventure story that will take any child into the past and will make them enter the Cathedral with eager enthusiasm...and trepidation.

Emma Bridgewater

Serpent / noun:

A snake, especially of a large kind

Serpentine / adjective:

Coiling, writhing, cunning, treacherous

Chapter One

The Antique Shop

The young traveller stumbled and fell to the cold stone floor. Thick yellow smoke clung to his clothes. It seemed to invade his very being. He had reached the point of total exhaustion. 'There must be a way out,' he cried in desperation, as he began searching frantically for the north door. 'I must get home, I must get home,' he began to chant under his breath as if to convince himself that all would be well.

Just as it seemed as if all hope was lost and that he would be banished here forever, he heard a clear, cold voice calling to him.

'Traveller, we three see you! You have entered the lair of the three serpents; what business do you have here?' The voice got louder and hissed with fury: 'Why have you disturbed us?'

Terrified, he looked up. The smoke vanished in an instant. Dragging himself to his feet he gasped in horror as he recognised the gruesome head and shimmering green eyes of a gigantic serpent leering down at him. The head was set in stone but it seemed to be alive. It had a quivering mouth and a set of sharp and vicious fangs that glistened menacingly. It hissed in the stillness. Below was a dark, heavy oak door cased with swirling metal patterns and set within a grand rounded stone arch.

'The north door', he whispered to himself, unwilling to provoke the serpent further. As he stood there frozen, he became aware of more sets of eyes piercing the gloom.

Two more stone serpent heads had appeared, one on either side of the scaly central figure. The two new serpents hissed their disapproval of the young man before them and added in unison: 'We are the guardians of the north door and we have been waiting for you. None shall pass below!!' There was a moment's pause and then all three yelled with fury. 'If you have no verse to give us then the north door will remain locked to you forever. You shall never travel homewards!'

At this, the traveller sank back to the floor. He knew that he had no verse to give them — it would be useless trying to battle his way through without it against such fearsome opponents. He began to sob bitterly as he realised that he would never see his home again. He was stranded here and at the serpents' mercy. The clues that he had so painstakingly pieced together during his journey here were useless now — they could not protect him and would certainly not get him home. Worst of all, he had failed in his mission; failed in the task he had been set. The serpents sensed this and began writhing and spitting with glee. The central head, goading him from above the north door itself, began to spin and twist, shaking itself menacingly. 'If you have no verse to give us then you must remain here forever.' It spat out the words with delight. The young man screamed as the head detached itself from the wall and came swooping down towards him, its long awful body trailing behind. The bulbous eyes of the serpent stared devilishly as it moved in for the kill. The traveller had only seconds...In a lightning flash, he remembered the small leather book and reached into his backpack to remove it. With a final desperate, heroic effort, he turned and flung the book as far away as possible, determined that it at least should escape the serpent.

He saw the piercing green eyes and dripping razor fangs as the jaws of the serpent closed in around him...

Thomas Buxton preferred to be called Tom. Most people he knew were happy with this, although one or two adults simply ignored his wish. He didn't like to make a fuss and quietly accepted that some things were unlikely to change, particularly as far as 'grown-ups' were concerned.

Tom lived in a small Victorian terraced house in one of the northern suburbs of Norwich. He shared it with his father, his sister Emma and his pet hamster Derek. He couldn't remember a time when his mother had been there. He knew that she must have existed at some point because there were pictures of her all over the house. Some of these showed him as a tiny baby being cradled in her loving arms. But he couldn't remember her smell, her laugh or in fact much about her at all. This upset him more than he would ever let on. There were rare occasions when his father had spoken about her, muttering simply that she had 'gone away.' Tom knew that the time was drawing near when this answer would no longer be good enough for him, but he was afraid of causing himself and his father pain by asking what had really happened to her. Yet there was one thing that he did know — and it was this. His sister Emma wore a silver locket around her neck, in which there were pictures of their youthful mother and father. Tom liked to think they were pictures of a couple who had just fallen in love. She never spoke about it, but he knew too that the pictures gave Emma comfort. He had noticed that in times of stress or when she was upset, she would touch the locket, playing with it almost subconsciously. This seemed to give her strength and encouragement, as if the locket and the pictures contained within had a power that helped her face and overcome the difficulty before her.

Ordinarily, the house would have been plenty big enough for the three of them (well, four if you include Derek the hamster), but Mr Buxton was a fanatical, obsessive collector of antiques. His antiques crowded and cluttered every square inch of space. Just why he was so obsessed the children never knew, but whatever the reason they found themselves constantly tripping over a puzzling and bizarre collection of objects. Edwardian bed pans, Zulu shields, miners' lamps, boxes of Victorian lacework — you name it and Mr Buxton was sure to have collected it. The house and its unusual contents were a source of constant embarrassment to the children, especially when friends came round to tea and ended up sitting down on a First World War tin pot helmet or tripping over the stacks of dusty books. Their only consolation was that Mr Buxton's particular obsession made buying him a Christmas present that much easier.

Tom Buxton supposed he was about average height for his age, with an average looking face and wore average kind of clothes. He didn't mind this – most of the time he rather enjoyed looking and acting just like everybody else around him, because things at home were so odd. He was quite a cautious child, and 'just in case' was one of his favourite expressions. He sort of liked going to school, but was determined not to admit it to anyone. He spent quite a lot of time at school all by himself. It had been during those times just recently that Tom had begun to wish that things were different. He may have lived in a house filled with peculiar things, but his life was, if he was honest with himself, actually rather dull. He wanted, just for once, to go on a journey far away from home. This journey would be full of adventure and would certainly be above average, he was sure of that. He had dreams about finding his mother, of rescuing her (from what he didn't know) and of bringing her safely home. And it was in these solitary moments that Tom somehow began to feel that this adventure actually would happen; it was just a question of when and where.

છ

Tom trudged reluctantly along Elm Hill – the ancient, cobbled medieval street that twists upwards towards the heart of the City. A flint built church stood crooked on the corner, giving way to art galleries, cafes and of course, any number of antique shops. Mr Buxton stopped outside one and shouted at no-one in particular; 'Pettus House! Home to the Pettus family from 1550 to 1683...'

Tom stifled a yawn as he followed rather begrudgingly towards the entrance. He stopped momentarily on the threshold and looked upwards to the shop name, etched in gold lettering on glass:

His sister Emma let out an audible sigh of boredom as she followed him inside, the jingle of the doorbell ringing behind.

'Ah, smell the history!' exclaimed Mr Buxton as he stood in the middle of the shop, sniffing loudly and blowing out large amounts of air. 'This is wonderful,' he boomed, 'the past comes alive!' And with that he marched off towards a great pile of tarnished brass pots and pans, knocking over a pair of olive wood candlesticks for good measure. Emma sighed again and picked up a cup and ball, trying to scoop the small wooden ball on a string back into the little cup in her hand. Tom wandered aimlessly towards the back of the shop.

He sort of liked learning about history; it was just that he wasn't really interested in all this stuff. Despite what his father said, it didn't seem to have any life in it at all. Anyway, their house was too full of things like this already. He looked at his watch anxiously — if they didn't move soon they would miss the river boat trip that was booked for later that afternoon. That would be typical.

Wandering further towards the rear of the shop, passing several dusty red tunics thrown carelessly over a chair, Tom thought he heard a peculiar sound. He stopped — it sounded something similar to a snake hissing. 'No, that's ridiculous,' he whispered to himself. 'This is an antique shop, not a pet store.' He listened. There it was again, definitely a hiss. He pushed his way past a rusty suit of armour which stood propped up against a window. The armour had turned various shades of brown and green with mouldy old age. The noise seemed to be coming from a collection of antique books which were stacked up on an old table ahead. He approached them cautiously, fascinated but slightly afraid. How could a book be hissing? Next to the pile of books was a faded sign, itself covered in cobwebs. The writing was faint;

Free to a Good Home — Please take one

Tom smiled to himself; 'Free to a cluttered home more like.' He picked up the book closest to him and blew the dust off its cover. He read the title out loud:

'A History of Dutch Clog Dancing: 1650 — 1700'

Fascinating I'm sure,' he murmured and replaced it. He began to glance through the others.

'*The Plague and How to Avoid It — 1300 to the Present Day*'

'*Tubs and Taps — The Story of the English Bathroom*'

He was beginning to think that he had imagined the whole thing. Or perhaps it was mice just scurrying amidst all this...all this... the word 'junk' popped into Tom's head. Almost despite himself, he studied the very last book on the table. It was the smallest and dirtiest of the lot. In fact it was covered with grime. As he picked it up and began to wipe the cover with his sleeve, strangely it let out a long and sinister hiss. Tom's fingers froze and he dropped it immediately. It was almost as if the book was trying to frighten him away — as if it didn't want to be picked up or even touched.

For a moment he thought about returning to the front of the shop and pretending that none of this had happened. He would probably find his father buying a pair of exhausted old boxing gloves then they could leave and never have to come back. Yet he was far too intrigued to do that. Nervously, he approached the book again and cautiously lifted it off the table. This time there was no hiss. He let out a sigh of relief and took the book over to the window for a better look. It had certainly seen better days. Its mottled cover was dark green and made of leather. Attached to the spine was a small and very fragile feather quill, its ink long since dried up. As he scraped away some of the dirt, Tom could just about make out a picture on the front cover. It seemed to be of a doorway, strong and impressive looking. It was set in a fine stone arch. Perhaps, he wondered, it led to a grand banqueting hall or was the entrance to some royal palace. Above the door were carvings in stone, but it was impossible to work out what they were. As far as he could tell, the book seemed to have no title.

He opened it carefully, wary that it might hiss again. The pages were tatty and brittle; he felt they might even disintegrate at his touch. There were spots of mould growing on them, but Tom could see that there were pictures inside, hurriedly sketched by some nervous hand. There was writing too, often just the odd word or sentence scribbled here and there, many of these followed by several exclamation marks. The very centre pages were missing. It seemed as if they had been torn out in a hurry as the remaining central spine was rough and uneven. He could just about decipher the words 'The Map of 12 – a map for your mission' written along the jagged spine of the ripped pages. And yet there was no map to be seen. Tom couldn't make any real sense of the book; the pages were far too ingrained with dirt for that. And yet something told him that this was a very old, very important book and that it had had many owners. He couldn't say why, but he felt that this book had travelled a great distance and had seen countless adventures. As he held it there in his hands, Tom felt as if this book already belonged to him.

As he closed the book and turned it over, he saw that a verse had been inscribed in the green leather on the back. The writing was far clearer than anything inside and it only took two quick wipes with his sleeve to read the rich golden lettering:

If you really want to return to before
you must face the three serpents of the north door.
A verse you will need to pass safely through
or the serpents will rage and devour both of you!

This made absolutely no sense to him, but he didn't much like the thought of being devoured by a serpent, which he was sure was some kind of gigantic and very ugly looking snake. As he contemplated this strange book in his hands, he heard a commotion coming from the front of the shop. 'Thomas! Emma! Come on, we're late, we're so, so late!' He turned to see his father come stumbling towards him, crashing into the rusty suit of armour as he went. 'Tom, there you are,' he panted. 'Good. Now quickly, come on — our river boat, we'll be late and miss it. We're supposed to launch in five minutes!' And with that he grabbed Tom by the arm and pulled him away from the table.

Much later, Tom realised that he had instinctively slipped the small green leather book inside his jacket pocket as they had rushed headlong out of the shop.

The 3 Serpents of the North Door

Chapter Two

The River Gatehouse

Five frantic minutes later and they were on the river Wensum. Mr Buxton was huffing and puffing for breath, attempting to row the boat and look cheerful all at the same time. Tom and Emma tried to ignore him. The best thing about their dramatic departure from the antique shop was that, for once, their father had failed to buy anything.

The children settled down to enjoy a slow, sun-soaked boat trip. Cotton wool clouds floated lazily across the clear blue sky and the faintest breeze rippled through the overhanging trees. They were determined to enjoy the time that was left to them before their return to school.

They both said publicly and categorically that they didn't want to go back to school, but if truth were told, they were looking forward to seeing their friends again and actually, they quite enjoyed some of their lessons and the things they learnt about. 'I think my favourite subject is history,' Tom mused, not noticing the broad smile breaking out on his father's face. Then thinking about it, he added 'and Mr Nicholas is okay, I suppose...I mean, for a teacher.'

'He does go on a bit though,' said Emma, who was only half listening. She had also become quite interested in the antique shop and had bought some smooth, sparkling gemstones. 'Trouble is –

do you think we'll end up like Dad?' she whispered to Tom, as she held up the shimmering coloured stones in the warm sunlight.

The boat drifted gently along, towards a right-hand bend in the river and the sturdy looking Cow Tower on the bank. This brick built structure seemed to be standing sentinel, guarding the City that lay behind it against any unwanted visitors. It was a strong defence against any would-be invaders.

And it caused Tom's mind to wander to the stories that Mr Nicholas had told them in class of the great Admiral Horatio Nelson and of the ferocious sea battles that he had fought so long ago. He began to imagine that their little rowing boat was the flagship of the fleet and that he, Tom Buxton, was its brave and fearless captain. Just as he began to scour the horizon for enemy ships, he heard his father shout something from the front of the boat. Had the enemy been spotted on the horizon? Should they take evasive action or prepare to attack?

Before he had the chance to ask his father to repeat the warning, Tom felt the air become instantly cold and damp around him. 'What's wrong?' Emma said worriedly as she moved closer to him in the boat. He wanted to reassure her that everything was fine, but he felt very unnerved himself. Their boat had very quickly become engulfed in a thick yellow fog. 'What the blazes is going on?' shouted Mr Buxton with a note of panic in his voice. 'How could it suddenly shroud over on a clear summer's day, it's simply not possible...' but his voice trailed off as a giant shape loomed suddenly out of the fog. It dwarfed their little vessel, but most terrifying of all, it was heading straight for them. 'What...

what is it?' stuttered Tom with fright. 'It doesn't look like an ordinary boat — maybe it's something else,' he gasped. No-one answered. 'Look out,' he yelled as it bore down, 'we're going to collide!' They clung desperately together for safety. The blackened, monstrous shape was almost upon them — it would surely smash their boat into a thousand pieces.

At the very last moment Tom peered above, half terrified of what he might see. It was unlike anything he had ever seen before; a magnificent wooden ship with huge, billowing white sails. There was very little breeze on the river, but these sails were full of wind; the ship pushed forcefully on by some mysterious, unknown force. There were many people on board; some of them were looking anxiously towards the little rowing boat, as if they too expected a collision and a great shattering of wood. But the ship whooshed past and just as quickly as it had appeared it was gone — off on its voyage to some distant land. 'River hog!' yelled Mr Buxton, shaking his fist, stumbling to his feet and in the process knocking an oar over the side. He watched helplessly as it floated tantalisingly out of reach. 'Blast!' he yelled in frustration, struggling as the boat bobbed dangerously to and fro on the swell that had been created. 'What was that?' exclaimed Emma. 'It almost smashed us to smithereens!' As Tom pondered the question, he wondered just exactly what cargo had been on board the gigantic boat and where it was going. 'Astonishing,' whispered their father from up ahead. 'The fog has lifted just as quickly as it came down. Come on,' he continued, 'we need to get ashore; we can't manage out here with only one oar.'

As they leant over the side and paddled for all they were worth, Tom noticed that his dad wasn't looking too well, a little — how might he describe it — seasick. Mr Buxton was sweating and cursing as he battled with the swell in an attempt to row to the nearest shore. Tom hadn't a clue where they were. 'Pull's Ferry!' Emma exclaimed as the boat clunked up to the shore with a dull thud. They clambered out into the cold water and began to haul it up the gangway. They decided instantly to rest on the grassy bank for a little while in order to regain their composure.

'Pull's... Pull's...what?' Tom murmured as he surveyed the building that stood close by. 'Pull's Ferry,' interrupted Mr Buxton impatiently, no doubt still flustered by his poor display of boating skills on the river. 'It was named after John Pull, the famous ferryman who used to live here.' He paused and looked around rather sheepishly. 'Or something like that anyway,' he shrugged. Tom was lost at this point — what was his Dad going on about? They had almost been crushed to death only minutes ago and here he was chattering on about some old ferryman. He started to wish he had never asked the question.

'I remember reading something about Mr Pull taking people across the river in his rowing boat,' Mr Buxton continued, gazing into the calming waters. 'Must've been difficult if he had a little boat like ours though, perhaps that's why he ran an inn for travellers here as well. You know, to keep a steady nerve and all.'

On cue, the creaking of an old pub sign drifted across to them as it swayed gently in the late summer breeze. The sign had seen better days for sure, its decrepit state indicating that the building it hung from had not served beer for a very long time. The building was made of flint, with a red tiled roof. It was missing a few, Tom noticed, and it seemed to be constructed around a great archway. To the right of the archway stood a small round flint tower, complete with defensive arrow slits.

'The Knights of the Window,' muttered Mr Buxton as he tried to read the sign. 'What an unusual name for an inn.' As they walked towards it, the sign creaked again and then fell silent. Tom could just about make out the image of three knights painted on to the wood. They seemed to be clad in green and brown armour and were carrying shields and lances. Yet the paint was so faded and weathered that it was difficult to distinguish them. Underneath in barely legible red lettering was written;

PROPRIETOR: Mr J. Postwick

Mr Buxton continued; 'Wasn't it through this archway that a great canal was dug? Much earlier than the inn of course.' He scratched his head and thought for a moment. 'Yes indeed — it was for the cargo boats coming up to build the new Cathedral. They unloaded the stone just up there. Yes, that's right,' he mused smugly, almost to himself, 'the stone came from Normandy I think.'

'But that's in France,' said Tom automatically and then stopped. Why on earth were they talking about this? Couldn't they just get home and forget about it all? And anyway, wouldn't it have been easier to use local stone, rather than bringing it all the way

over from France?

His dad continued, 'the imported stone was of far better quality than anything we have here Tom; most of the Cathedral was built from it. Like I said, I think it was transported on huge cargo boats along the river and then through this archway at Pull's Ferry. The builders could then take the stone right up to the construction site itself.' Tom shivered slightly — hadn't he seen large pieces of gleaming white stone on the boat that had almost smashed into them back on the river?

The creaking of a door interrupted these thoughts and they turned in unison to see light streaming from one side of Pull's Ferry. Tom was shocked to realise that dusk was falling. A slightly stooped, frail old man came hobbling through the door and approached them, crunching his way slowly across the gravel. He certainly cut a bizarre figure. He was shorter than any of them and wore a filthy old red jacket with tarnished brass buttons down the front. It was quite like one of the tunics that Tom had seen earlier that morning, flung carelessly over a chair in the antique shop. Emma noticed that some of the buttons were missing, but declined to mention this to the stooped figure. The man's trousers were more like shorts and were striped, but what colour they were could only be guessed at because they seemed to have centuries worth of dirt encrusted upon them. And the man had the most peculiar of moustaches — grey, bushy and curling upward at each end. The children had never seen anything like it.

'Mr...Mr...Pull?' asked Emma nervously, saying the first thing that had come in to her head. 'No,' the man chuckled, 'no...no...no... I'm Mr Postwick the present gatekeeper. John Pull hasn't lived here for... oh let me see now, at least 150 years.' Emma and Tom shot each other a quick glance. Mr Postwick chuckled again, 'I saw your little shipwreck; looked terrible. Maybe a cup of tea and a slice of cake will set your nerves straight.'

After the trauma of their near miss on the river, the prospect of a cup of tea was certainly very attractive. It drew all three of them into following Mr Postwick. As they walked to the right of the impressive flint tower, Tom glanced back at the river once again. It was still, silent and gloomy.

Just ahead of them was a small wooden door, which Tom judged to be about half the size of a normal doorway. It was in a very bad state of repair and looked as if it might fall off its hinges at any moment. The gatekeeper disappeared through it and Mr Buxton stooped to follow. 'Come on kids — it's fine,' he just had time to say before he stood up too early and whacked his head on the low ceiling, sending several pieces of rotten wood tumbling to the floor. 'Blast!' he shouted, as Emma suppressed a giggle.

Inside, the gatehouse was dark and cool. A thick layer of dust covered all the surfaces – it was as if nothing had been moved or touched for centuries. Tom and Emma didn't find it frightening; after all, they were used to strange houses. Yet here it wasn't simply a collection of dusty and dirty old objects and furniture - it was as if everything had been frozen, that time itself had stood still. Tom had the distinct feeling that the house and its contents, maybe even time itself, were waiting for something, or someone, to start it again.

Mr Postwick stood at the entrance to the sitting room and ushered them in with a proud grin on his face. 'Sit here, dear friends, sit' he said, pointing to a rather decrepit looking sofa which was pushed back against the wall. Above it was the only window, grimy and covered in cobwebs. 'I've been waiting for you,' he chuckled, placing a small oil lamp on a table. 'Been a long time since travellers have passed this way.' Mr Buxton frowned, but before he could speak, the old man continued. 'Tea and cake it is then,' he smiled and scurried off towards the kitchen. As they heard the clinking of tea cups and plates, the visitors were able to take stock of their surroundings. 'This is the oddest place I've ever seen,' said Mr Buxton, adjusting the lamp so that it gave off more light. Emma raised an eyebrow. 'Fascinating though, isn't it?' he added as an afterthought. Tom couldn't disagree. Aside from the sofa, the only other pieces of furniture in the room were an old rocking chair, its tatty and torn fabric spilling out everywhere, and an equally tired looking table, which stood proudly in the centre. Yet the strangest thing about the room was its walls. They were covered with clocks, watches and timepieces of all shapes, sizes and descriptions. There were large grandfather clocks and little wooden cuckoo clocks. There were pocket watches dangling down on chains and even sundials made from brass that looked as if they had been nailed hurriedly into place. Square, circular and triangular clocks all jostled for position. And yet there was no ticking and chiming at all. Every clock and timepiece hung there silently; none of them appeared to be working. Interspersed amongst these clocks were one or two very faded portraits that appeared to have suffered from years of neglect. Curious, Tom rose from the sofa and studied the one closest to him. A boyish, smiling face peered back. 'Nathaniel somebody or other' Tom reported, squinting at the tiny engraving in the bottom right hand corner. He moved away to inspect the odd assortment of clocks and timepieces.

Emma too was on her feet, and had hurriedly cleaned several of the clocks. 'They're all stuck at different times,' she announced puzzled. She looked down at her own watch. Oddly, it too had stopped. She tapped it and checked again. The hands had definitely stopped moving and there was no ticking at all. It had come to a halt at seven minutes past seven o'clock. 'Dad,' she whispered, 'my watch, it's…' But her voice trailed off as she turned to see her father fast asleep, mouth gaping, on the rickety old rocking chair. 'Probably the excitement on the river,' she mumbled as Mr Postwick bounced back into the room.

'Careful now, do be careful!' the gatekeeper muttered to himself as he tried desperately to avoid spilling the tea. He spotted Mr Buxton asleep and smiled. 'Ah, that always happens to the adults,' he said with a hint of mischief in his voice. 'He'll sleep through it all now I expect' he chuckled, putting the tea tray down and turning to face the children.

They both dived towards the food, for it had been quite a while since they had last eaten. Despite stuffing several large pieces of chocolate cake into his mouth, Tom managed to puff out a question.

'Er...um...Mr Postwick,' he said, consuming as much tea and cake as possible, 'why do none of these clocks or watches actually work?'

The gatekeeper's face lit up in a broad smile.

'That's the question I've been hoping you would ask,' he replied, 'to start it all off.' He stood perfectly still and upright in the centre of the room. 'I need you both you see, help on the adventure, what with the rescue mission and all...'

Tom looked quizzically across to Emma and then back to Mr Postwick.

'Oh I'll be there too, don't worry,' he said... I might just be a little...well, how can I put it...diminished, you know, in size. Help as best I can though. You see I'm here all alone and I need him back. And I need you two to help me get him. Terribly important stuff this you know, creating the City of Light. Now you both might want to hold on to something secure,' he continued, the moustache twitching anxiously at the corners of his mouth.

The words had only just escaped his lips when from somewhere there came an incredibly loud bang, just like a shotgun going off. Both children jolted with fright and ducked down for cover, forgetting the refreshments in an instant. At once, every clock, watch and timepiece on the walls of the sitting room sprang into life. The children stared in wonderment as the whirring, spinning and ticking of so many clocks erupted from the walls. Some timepieces reached their hour marks and began to chime, which only added to the confusion. Thunderous bells, like those of a Cathedral belfry, boomed out across the room and were joined by a multitude of jingles, jangles, chimes and crashes. Tiny cuckoos sprang from their nests and chirped away hastily before retreating into their little wooden houses. The hands of the clocks were not all following the same pattern either – some were zooming around at a hundred miles an hour whilst others seemed to be lazily performing their task. Some of the hands were going in a clockwise direction, as they should of course, but others had decided to be difficult and were heading the other way. Tom looked again to Emma who shook her head in puzzlement. It was a scene of utter bewilderment. As Tom spun around the room, he began to feel light-headed. The activity, noise and sheer strangeness of the scene were overpowering. He staggered over to the sofa, where he managed to slump down in a dizzying heap. And then as quickly as the clocks had sprung in to life, they stopped; all together and at the same precise moment.

Everything stood still and silent for a second.

'Amazing,' said Emma, hurriedly reporting the situation. 'They've all stopped at seven minutes past seven, despite what they were doing – that's the same time as...' Yet before she could finish her sentence, what can only be described as a deep groan came from the very walls of the room itself. Emma shot over to Tom, who instinctively reached out for her. The groan was followed by a great grinding and churning, as if giant cogs that had lain dormant for centuries were finally being mustered into life. Tom glanced over to his father, but he was still fast asleep, his mouth wide open and catching flies. The noise grew ever louder and as Tom listened intently, he thought he heard the sound of huge, heavy iron chains being dragged over cold, wet stone. There also came the sound of steam escaping – an intermittent hiss that burst through the relentless grinding of the cogs and chains. And then as the terrible noise reached its awful crescendo, the sitting room itself began to shake. At first it just rattled the clocks and portraits on the walls, but very quickly the sofa, rocking chair and table were all moving uncontrollably.

'What's happening?' yelled Emma in panic. But Tom had no answer. He had his eyes tightly shut. He wanted, more than anything, to be away from this spinning, dizzying, terrifying room. From behind his eyes there suddenly came a light. A blinding, intense white light that he knew would burn like the sun. He opened his eyes, but the light had obliterated the room completely. He could not escape it. As he pleaded for it to be gone, Tom heard a voice – the voice of Mr Postwick – calling from somewhere up ahead. He listened intently, as if it were the last thing he had to hold on to;

Your question has triggered the ticking of time,
that can only be stopped by obtaining the rhyme.
As for me I will help where I can and I must,
for I am a companion in whom you can trust!

Chapter Three

The Clock-Jack

The two children huddled together for comfort, afraid and unsure as to what had just happened to them. The silence which engulfed them was complete. It was in total contrast to the ear splitting noise and dizzying panic they had just experienced. Tom struggled to his feet and again surveyed the scene; the intense white light had vanished and had been replaced by the half-light of dawn. His dizziness had cleared and he took stock of the situation. They ought to be standing, he reasoned, in the sitting room of the river gatehouse. But that too had gone and under their feet was damp, cold grass. It was also quite clear that it was only the two of them that had arrived at this place – wherever that was. Gone was the diminutive Mr Postwick and their father too was nowhere to be seen. Emma clutched Tom's hand, yet he was unable to summon any words to comfort her. He noticed that with her other hand she was absentmindedly touching the silver locket around her neck.

'Where are we Tom, what happened?' she pleaded, her voice wobbling with fear. He couldn't answer and simply shook his head.

They began to move on instinct, frightened and alone, wanting to get as far away from that place as possible. Further and further they went, moving all the time away from the river. Confused and dazed, they stumbled onwards as icy fingers of daylight began to claw their way through the grey dawn.

Then faintly, ever so quietly in the distance, they heard sounds of activity — clinking and clanging, beating and hammering. They slowed to a cautious walk. There were voices too — many voices in conversation, growing steadily louder and louder until at last, as the final residues of the night disappeared, they saw it. They gasped at what lay before them. Stretched out into the distance and surrounding them on all sides were hundreds and hundreds of people, all busily at work, yelling instructions and commands, rushing this way and that and all, it appeared, working together on some great common task. It was a scene of furious industry and activity.

As the children advanced upon the scene cautiously, they saw many men unloading large pieces of cut white stone from huge wooden boats into great reed baskets. These baskets were then being lifted up and on to the muddy bank. The tethered boats bobbed to and fro on a narrow canal that snaked its way into the distance. Other men were directing the stone filled baskets into sturdy wagons and carts that were ready to be pulled by oxen. Giant piles of stones stood dotted around, with some of the workers leaning up against them, smiling, chatting and taking a break from their difficult work. Several women were wandering amongst the workers, offering refreshment. Emma and Tom gazed at the scene and looked at one another in amazement. 'What... what is this place?' Tom pleaded, 'Where's Dad and Mr...Mr Postwick. What's happened?'

'And,' added Emma, 'why has no-one noticed us? I mean look at our clothes — we stand out a mile!'

That was certainly true — their jackets, t-shirts, jeans and trainers were at complete odds with the rough woollen tunics and leather sandals worn by those around them. Emma seemed intrigued, the shock of their recent experience seemingly now lost on her. Tom watched as her gaze followed the plodding oxen, as they hauled the carts slowly away from the boats. He saw her squint as the carts grew smaller and smaller in the distance and then jumped as she cried out. She had seen their final destination. 'They're...they're...' she whispered, unable to believe what she was seeing...'They're building the Cathedral!'

Now Tom Buxton wasn't stupid – he knew that. He would freely admit that his mind wandered sometimes when Mr Nicholas went waffling on about some tedious historical facts and their impact on the civilised world...blah, blah, blah. Yet even Tom knew that Norwich Cathedral had been built a long, long time ago, that it was in fact hundreds of years old and that ... well, they couldn't be constructing it now because it had already been built! 'For goodness sake,' he retorted angrily, allowing his eyes to focus on what Emma was staring at. 'Be serious.' She was usually so sensible.

Tom stared into the middle distance. He blinked, shook his head and stared again. Incredibly, Emma appeared to be right! As his eyes followed the many carts trundling away, he could see a great building on the horizon, silhouetted in the early morning sun. This magnificent structure was shrouded in wooden scaffolding and rose majestically skywards as if it was clawing at the heavens. It was the unmistakable sight of their Cathedral under construction and he recognised it immediately.

In a state of shock, Tom leant against a large pile of cut stone.

His mind was racing. 'How could this be? How could this be?' Norwich Cathedral had been built over nine hundred years ago and yet here they were, Tom and Emma Buxton, standing in broad daylight and watching it being built! And why, despite all these people and all this activity, had he and his sister not been noticed? He sat down to ponder these baffling questions. In doing so, he glanced over at a small pile of rubble only a few metres away.

He could see something unusual propped up against it. It looked like a tiny person, lying motionless amidst the debris. He motioned to Emma to follow him as he got up and approached it cautiously— Tom wasn't sure he could take many more shocks. They found a carved wooden figure, quite small — but brightly painted, lying still amongst the rubble, wood and bits of old scaffolding.

The figure was incredibly odd. On its head a small golden helmet rested on a shock of thick, curly black hair. Its red face looked as if it were blushing. A sharp pointed nose stood out over a thick black moustache which Tom thought was curling upward slightly at each end. The figure wore a red tunic and striped short trousers — the stripes were quite faded, but Tom could make out that the colours were yellow and green. He couldn't help but smile at this because his favourite football team, Norwich City, wore the same colours (although their shorts were not quite so dirty and faded). He experienced a momentary feeling of familiarity — a rare and welcome thing in their present surroundings. On its feet the figure wore small black shoes with golden buckles and thick brown woolly socks. Most peculiar of all was the fact that although the figure was lying motionless, it appeared to be quietly ticking away to itself.

'I think that's a Clock-Jack' whispered Emma, 'they're used to decorate one of the great clocks here at the Cathedral. Dad's always wanted one for his collection — he's never stopped going on about it.' She looked thoughtful. 'I didn't know they actually existed though.' Tom studied the little figure with interest. There was something strangely familiar about the little Clock-Jack's face, but he couldn't quite put his finger on it. What totally surprised him was the way that the Clock-Jack suddenly smiled and winked at him. Emma took a step backwards as it turned its head to wink at her as well. What followed was even more surprising. The little figure shook its head, smiled again and sat up. Dusting down its smart red tunic, it sprang quickly to its feet, pointed at them and started to sing:

Ha! Time travellers here I see,
now I will be your guide for free;
all you must do is guess my name
to join me in this merry game!

The Clock-Jack stopped his singing and shifted his glance from Tom to Emma, shuffling his feet impatiently in the dirt. Tom tried not to laugh at the high pitched squeal of his singing voice and raised a hand to his mouth to cough.

But Emma was distracted; 'Time travellers?' she whispered, struggling with the thought. The Clock-Jack didn't hear and smiled confidently as if there was no way in the world that anyone could guess his name. 'Um ... er ... is it ... er ... Jack, by any chance?' she asked, regaining her composure. The Clock-Jack huffed and puffed and stamped his feet. He seemed rather upset at Emma's suggestion. Now he sang again, but this time his voice growled with anger:

It is, so now our travels will start,
In this epic tale you must be of strong heart.
The centuries will pass on our journey through time,
— make sure you are listening to each little rhyme!

And with that he sprang forward, grabbing Emma's arm and drawing her close. He hissed under his breath:

If you really want to return to before
you must face the three serpents of the north door.
A verse you will need to pass safely through
or the serpents will rage and devour both of you!

A distant memory of that verse swam through Tom's head, but for now his attention was focused on the way that the Jack was gripping Emma tightly. She seemed in pain and Tom didn't like it. He moved with a start and just as he was about to wrestle her free, the little Clock-Jack let go and scampered across the rubble at quite a pace. He was heading in the direction of the new Cathedral.

Chapter Four

Jack – A Trusted Companion?

They felt that they had no option but to follow – the Jack was after all the only person (or thing) that had noticed them. In no time at all they were nearing the great Cathedral building itself. They could now see clearly many of its beautifully decorated columns, arches and windows. It was even busier here than it had been near the boats and the children found it difficult to follow Jack as he darted onwards. There were men dressed in bright, coarse looking woollen clothing rushing around doing all sorts of jobs. And it looked hard, physical work. Some were finishing and decorating the great pieces of stone and carefully placing them in huge baskets to be lifted up to those workers standing on the upper levels. Others were digging foundations for new walls, whilst yet more were lashing together wooden poles to form the scaffolding that encased the building in its giant cage. And all the time all around them was the constant clinking rhythm of hammer and chisel on stone.

Tom didn't much like the look of the wooden scaffolding – it seemed rather flimsy and unsafe, as if it could come crashing down at any moment. He turned pale when Jack motioned for them to follow and began to climb, seemingly without a care, up on to the scaffolding itself. Emma followed nervously and Tom, not wanting to be left on his own, reluctantly did the same. They climbed higher and higher – up into the clouds it seemed – until they finally came to rest on the very top wooden plank. Tom clutched an upright support pole for safety and squinted out of the corner of his eye.

It was a breathtaking scene. From their vantage point they could see across the city of Norwich, although it was much smaller in size than the city that Emma and Tom were familiar with. They saw the great motte and bailey castle, built from similar looking stone as that of the Cathedral. They could just about make out the soldiers on guard duty, patrolling high up on the battlements. They could also see the river, crowded with many boats of varying sizes and colours. Tom's heart leapt and then sank immediately — there was no trace of Pull's Ferry and the river gatehouse.

He looked over at Emma, who clutched his hand in reassurance. 'What did Jack mean about having to face the three serpents if we want to return to before?' he whispered. 'Is it how we get back to Dad? And what was all that about needing a verse?'

'Didn't he say something about us both being devoured?' she replied anxiously. Tom didn't want to think too much about that — his colour was only just returning. Then it came back to him.....

'The book!' he yelled at the top of his voice, digging deep in to his pocket to find it. The scaffolding wobbled.

'What?'

'That's where I read the rhyme Emma,' he shouted in a state of agitation - 'in the book I picked up in that boring old shop.' Although it didn't seem quite such a boring old shop to him now. As he retrieved the small leather book and hurriedly flicked through it, Tom noticed a remarkable thing. Where it had once been dusty, dirty and encased in grime, the book now shone as if it were brand new. Its smart green leather cover was newly bound and the small feather quill glistened with fresh ink on its tip. Yet he paid little attention to that, quickly turning it over to look at the back. 'There,' he said, pointing in triumph. 'There it is – the rhyme I mean.' Sure enough, staring back at them in fine golden lettering was the rhyme that Jack had spoken only minutes ago:

If you really want to return to before
you must face the three serpents of the north door.
A verse you will need to pass safely through
or the serpents will rage and devour both of you!

'Who does it belong to?' asked Emma.

'Who does what belong to?'

'The book of course, stupid!'

'Oh…um…I don't know' he replied, 'I hadn't thought of that. Let's see.'

He turned the book over and opened it. The pages were creamy white and new, not brittle and covered with green mould as they had been before. On the first page it said:

'I wonder who he is?' whispered Emma as Tom carefully turned the next page.

'Whoever he is...or was,' muttered Tom, 'he's already met Jack — look!'

Emma grabbed the book from him. There on the second page was a sketch, as clear as anything, of the little Clock-Jack they had just met and who was now in fact sitting only a few metres away from them.

Jack, a trusted companion~of sorts!

'Jack – a trusted companion – of sorts!' repeated Emma, reading from the book and then frowning across at Jack. 'Tom I don't get it. Where did you find this book? Who was this Nathaniel Rowbottom and how did he know Jack? What does this all mean?'

'Look,' Tom replied quickly, his mind racing. 'This Nathaniel guy must have been here in this place before. He calls himself a time traveller on the first page. That's what Jack called us too! Nathaniel must have met with Jack at some point. Maybe he wrote down what he did and who he met in this book. He kept a record of everything he encountered!' Tom frantically scanned some of the drawings and text contained in the book. 'Perhaps we really are time travellers as well,' he continued hesitantly. 'Emma, this book could be really useful for us; remember Jack said he was going to take us on some sort of journey through time...' His voice trailed off. This was certainly a lot to take in.

'Maybe we can add things to it,' whispered Emma pointing to the quill. 'With that I mean.'

Tom ignored her. 'But why are we here?' he said quietly. 'I mean, what's the point of it?' And all these people that we've seen, are they real or are they...' he was unable to suppress a shiver, 'are they... ghosts?' His voice drained away to nothingness.

Jack had been paying them no attention whatsoever, but now became very excited and leapt to his feet. Tom hurriedly put the book away. The Clock-Jack was shouting and pointing into the Cathedral itself. He jumped up and down so hard that he began to make the scaffolding wobble and caused some dust to shake loose from the stones next to them.

Sensing that it wouldn't be too clever to fall off the scaffolding from such a great height, Emma tried to calm him down; 'Jack,' she said calmly. It had no effect. 'Jack!!' she screamed at the top of her voice. That seemed to do the trick as the Clock-Jack sat down immediately and turned to look at her. 'I know you're excited,' she continued, 'but you almost shook us off the plank here. Tell us what you can see.'

'Bishop Herbert,' Jack replied immediately and smiled:

Bishop Herbert de Losinga in 1096
founded this Cathedral with mortar and bricks;
now it is here to God's great glory
follow me on and discover its story

They followed a little further along the plank so that they could see more clearly what was happening below. Bishop Herbert de Losinga was leading a great procession of men wearing long black cloaks and hoods.

'This is really weird,' muttered Tom. 'Do you think this actually *is* the year 1096?'

'I don't know,' said Emma, 'it doesn't make any sense. But somehow we are here – or at least we think we are...'

Tom gazed to the floor below. He guessed the men in the cloaks must be monks, men who spent their lives working and worshipping here at the Cathedral. As the procession came to a halt before the altar, he counted about thirty monks altogether.

The monks lowered their hoods

and all looked towards Bishop Herbert. The Bishop smiled at them and then turned to climb the steps behind the altar. He sat down on a large stone chair and raised his head towards the rafters. 'That's the Cathedra,' whispered Emma.

Tom looked at her blankly. 'The Cathedra,' she continued, 'it's the ancient name for the Bishop's seat – it's why this whole building is called a Cathedral.'

Before he had time to say that if he'd wanted an RE lesson he would have asked for one, Tom felt Jack bouncing up and down again, squeaking with delight. The little wooden figure was waving and singing to the Bishop:

Bishop Herbert look at me.
It's Jack, your friend, can't you see?

Fat chance of that thought Tom, you're only a metre tall and you're stuck right up here in the clouds. But amazingly Bishop Herbert turned his head towards Jack, his face lighting up in a broad and affectionate smile. Jack's tunic almost burst with pride as the Bishop waved at him before focussing his attention once more on the monks and the task in hand.

As Tom followed Jack's gaze he noticed that each of the monks was carrying a candle. The light from the candles illuminated the great columns, arches and pillars around them. The light danced on the stonework, and he saw how beautifully decorated the Cathedral was. Every last stone was painted with bright reds, yellows, pinks and greens – a whole rainbow of colours. Emma too had become transfixed by the sight before them. She was trying to ignore Jack, who was becoming excited again:

The Bishop and monks are ready to pray
to give thanks for this wonderful day.
The Cathedral is ready so let us begin
to welcome the people – let them come in!

At this the monks all looked up to the rafters and let out a great shout of joy. They then started to sing in what seemed like a rather strange language. In times like this (in other words when he was feeling confused or unsure), Tom often turned to his sister. So he looked at Emma, but for once she seemed just as puzzled as he was. He started to feel light-headed again. What was happening to them exactly? How had they come from a peaceful river cruise with their father to find themselves sitting on top of some rickety old scaffolding watching the Bishop and his monks praying in Norwich Cathedral? Was this really the year 1096? And how might Nathaniel Thingeywhatsit's ancient book play a part in all of this?

Tom began to feel a gathering sense of dread rising up within him. If only he was back at home playing football with his friends. Or maybe he'd just wake up and find himself all cosy and warm in his bed. He closed his eyes tightly, waiting and hoping for that to happen. But it didn't. Instead, all that came swimming into his mind was the echo of Jack's sinister rhyme, written so clearly on the back of the antique book:

But if you really want to return to before
you must face the three serpents of the north door.
A verse you will need to pass safely through
or the serpents will rage and devour both of you!

Tom shuddered as a ghostly image drifted before him. He saw the figure of a young man who seemed to be somewhere in a building very much like this one. It may well even have been this Cathedral. Tall columns and arches dwarfed the figure on either side. The man fell to his knees and shouted something in anguish, yet Tom heard no sound. 'Nathaniel,' he whispered instinctively. The man looked frantically all around as if desperate for escape. It was clear that he was trapped and terrified. Tom screamed in horror as he saw three menacing shadows envelop the figure on his knees. Without warning the young man was devoured by a powerful, terrifying serpent, its razor sharp teeth cutting and hissing with glee. Tom wrenched himself away from this nightmarish scene.

He opened his eyes and felt his clammy forehead. His clothes were drenched with sweat. The vision he had just experienced was so awful. It was made even more so by the dawning realisation that he had just seen one of the three serpents and that its victim had been the time traveller, Nathaniel Rowbottom.

He looked hurriedly around for Emma and Jack and was startled to find himself shrouded in a gathering mist. He realised that he was still sitting at the very top of the Cathedral. Yet this time he was not sitting on a rickety old plank of wood but on a smooth and firm piece of stone. He ran his hand along it. The scaffolding had vanished. He glanced around to find everything was quiet and still. Bishop Herbert and the monks had all disappeared and the Cathedral was silent. He could just about make out the brightly painted walls and ceiling, but they were different somehow. It was as if all the great building work that they had seen earlier had been finished and the Cathedral was now complete. He turned to tell Emma of his terrifying vision but both she and Jack had also disappeared. He began to panic. It was happening again. 'Please don't let me be here all on my own,' Tom whispered to himself, 'please, not here, not now...'

Chapter Five

Riot!

Tom heard a very faint and distant call. 'Tom! Tom! Come on.'
It came again. 'Tom – come on! We're down here. Hurry!' He
looked for the direction of the voice but could not see very far.
The mist was still thick around him. He recognised the voice as
Emma's and thought it was coming from the floor of the
Cathedral. So he began his descent, climbing down carefully for
what seemed like ages. The scaffolding had gone – Tom descended
countless stone steps, spiralling down to the left. The immense
size and scale of the place overwhelmed him. He felt like a tiny
flea. Yes, a flea inside a giant's house as he imagined a great giant
lurching its way through the countless arches and doorways.

When he finally reached the ground, Tom let out a sigh of
relief as he saw Emma and Jack standing not too far in front of
him. It was an odd sight to see his sister
holding the little Clock-Jack's hand and
Jack, all buttoned up and beaming in his
smart red tunic. Any hostility that Jack had
shown them when they had first met now
seemed to have disappeared entirely. He
reached up to grab Tom's hand and led
them both eagerly into a great open space
in the belly of the building. Tom felt he

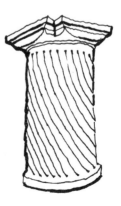

had been here before on some distant occasion, yet that was of little comfort to him now.

As he looked around, Tom could see pictures and patterns painted all over the Cathedral walls and ceiling, but he had no time to view them properly. Jack didn't allow them to stop. He led them skipping and running right through huge open doors, bringing them to a halt outside the Cathedral itself. He was certainly in a good mood – a mood that was far removed from the uneasiness the children themselves were feeling. Jack quickly piped up:

Get ready for the riot of 1272
of flaming fury and destruction too;
the fires will rage and burn so bright
so come with me to watch this sight!

'We've moved on in time,' said Emma quickly. 'Almost two hundred years, that's if Jack is telling the truth. I didn't even notice.'

'You don't seem to have aged,' Tom interjected with a half-smile.

Emma paid no attention and checked her watch, but it still wasn't working. It was stuck, just as it had been at the river gatehouse. She echoed the time it showed; 'Seven minutes past seven.'

'The Cathedral seems such a peaceful and calm place right now,' pondered Tom, more concerned for their safety than for anything else. 'What did Jack say about a riot?'

His question was rudely answered as a flaming arrow shot high in the sky, arched over and then come whizzing down towards them, whooshing through the cold night air. It seemed to have come from somewhere beyond the well built walls of the Cathedral grounds. 'Look out!' Tom cried, diving desperately for cover. The arrow had fallen just short of them, but was quickly followed by several more, every one of which thudded into a wooden building that stood close by. They watched with horror as the building quickly caught alight; red, yellow and orange flames engulfing the dry wood. 'Jack!' Emma yelled, 'what's happening – who is attacking the Cathedral?' But this time the Clock-Jack had no answer and scampered quickly away. 'He's left us,' Emma stood, open mouthed.

Tom was sure that all the arrows were coming from beyond the Cathedral walls; he could hear a great mass of people out there shouting in anger and rage. It was a furious sound, like a great storm – raging, crashing and unstoppable. Seeking shelter as more and more flaming arrows were shot into the air towards them, the children managed to locate Jack sheltering behind a clump of sturdy yew trees. The massive canopy of branches was silhouetted against the night sky and it afforded them some cover.

From this relative safety they were able to see all that was happening. The huge crowd of angry people burst through the gates that had been locked against them and were streaming into the Cathedral grounds. Many of them were carrying spears and poles; some held flaming torches whilst others seemed to be wielding swords and clubs. Tom shuddered as he realised that almost everyone in the crowd carried a weapon of some sort. Astonishingly, the mob started to attack the Cathedral; some fired flaming arrows towards the Cloister, the four connected walkways attached to the side of the main Cathedral building. Others attacked the bell tower where defenders loyal to the Cathedral were hurling arrows and rocks down on their attackers.

It was a terrifying scene and as he watched the events develop, Tom tried to think of exactly why a violent riot like this might have started and how they might be able to get away from it. Lost in thought, he failed to notice one of the rioters break away from the main group and head directly towards them. Only too late did they try to make themselves invisible behind the trees but it was of no use – the rioter had spotted them.

'Do you work for the Bishop?' he roared with fury as he approached, his face reddened with anger. When no answer was forthcoming he bellowed again. 'Are you in the pay of this greedy, grasping Bishop?' The rioter clutched a very sharp looking scythe and swung it menacingly in their direction. It sliced through the cold air. Tom shook his head silently, too terrified to speak. He had noticed a twisted, gnarled serpent badge pinned to the man's cloak. 'No matter,' barked the rioter. 'No matter indeed, for this is the last time that the Bishop demands more money from us!' He howled, spat on the ground and shook his fist at the Cathedral. 'How can we afford to pay such rents for our markets in Tombland? Our families are starving!'

With that he threw his scythe to the ground and, drawing the bow from his back, shot an arrow with a great whoosh towards the Cloister. Tom watched it climb high in the air and followed as it came zooming down to lodge itself in the wooden roof. A great cheer went up from the crowd and two or three burning arrows followed. Together these arrows helped to set the Cloister roof alight. The orange and yellow flames spread quickly, crackling and spitting as they went and lighting up the night sky. Tom couldn't help but gasp in amazement to see such glorious colours and the dancing of the flames as they reached ever higher and higher. Sparks whizzed and crackled like a hundred fireworks all taking off at once as the Cloister was engulfed in the rampant fire.

The fire fizzed through any wooden structure it could find, destroying everything in its path and creating huge clouds of thick black smoke. Gradually the clouds began to shroud the scene before them. Tom turned back to face the rioter, but he had gone to rejoin the seething mass of discontented citizens. Tom could taste the acrid smoke in his throat, drying him out and suffocating. He rubbed his eyes as they became reddened and sore. He stumbled over towards Emma; she too was choked by the densely packed clouds. Tom spluttered and cried out to her, yet felt himself becoming dizzy once more as everything became black around them...

Chapter Six

A Familiar Face

Tom awoke to find himself lying flat on his back and staring up at a clear blue sky. Next to him, Jack and Emma were picking themselves up and dusting down their clothes. Soot and ash had covered them and even lined the folds and creases of their skin.

'A hot shower would be nice,' muttered Emma.

'We survived,' Tom answered. His mind was a million miles away from such creature comforts.

He struggled to his feet and took in the scene around them. The giant yew trees had gone and they were right in the centre of the Cloister on the lush green grass. Yet the Cloister itself was not a smouldering pile of ash and debris, but rather four grand stone covered walkways, joining together once again to form the huge square. They looked solid and magnificent and very unlikely to burn in any flaming riot. And there were sounds of construction activity again — the familiar, yet this time more delicate chinking and clinking of hammer and chisel on stone. As they approached the sound, Jack started to sing:

Masons rebuilt the Cloister so grand
and carved so well — the best in the land!
So come now see the masons' design
a beautiful roof boss so splendid and fine.

'Hey Tom,' breezed Emma, 'do you remember those roof boss postcards you were sent?'

'Roof boss...' started Tom rather absentmindedly – he was carefully leafing through the antique book; perhaps there were pictures of such things drawn inside. But he found none, only one or two nonsensical sentences and an unnerving sketch of the top half of a smiling skeleton. He turned his attention to his sister's question. 'What? Oh yeah, carvings you mean – pictures, yeah I do remember those postcards. Didn't Dad send them to me from a Cathedral he'd visited in the north?' He didn't let on that he was struggling to really remember what roof bosses actually were.

'No, I'm sure they were from here,' Emma continued, reaching the Cloister walkway. As she said this, Tom felt a sudden upswing in his mood. All thoughts of facing serpents and getting through north doors had, for now at least, left his mind. He smiled as it came flooding back to him. His dad had written, rather too excitedly Tom felt, about how the roof bosses were carved high into the vaulted ceiling of the building and how they were designed to help people understand the message of the Bible more easily. That's right – each one told a little story – 'a story in stone' was his father's phrase. There were some bosses however that appeared to

be far removed from any Bible story. Images of dragons, dancers, green-men and seven-headed beasts began to swim through Tom's mind.

He had particularly liked the postcard showing the roof boss of the Egyptian Pharaoh drowning in the Red Sea. The stonemason had given the Pharaoh a shining suit of golden armour and this had made him look more like a medieval knight than a Biblical king. Mr Buxton, expert on such antiquities of course, had written that this was probably because the stonemason had never actually seen a real Egyptian Pharaoh because he lived in Norfolk — an answer that Tom reluctantly agreed made a lot of sense. He became quite excited at the possibility of seeing an actual stonemason at work now. Perhaps it was the same mason that had made the Pharaoh roof boss and then Tom could test his Dad's theory and ask him whether or not he had actually been to ancient Egypt.

They found the stonemason perched expertly at the top of a wooden ladder in one of the Cloister walkways. He was deep in concentration, smoothing and dusting the stone he had recently cut. The vaulting here was quite low — easily close enough for them to get a good look at the carved image that appeared to be nearing completion. There were two figures — a young boy and an old woman and the boy seemed to be attempting to snatch away items

of clothing the woman had recently washed on her old wooden scrubbing board. Yet this washer woman was far too quick for the young thief and had grabbed him by the scruff of the neck. Her right arm was raised as if to deliver an almighty blow to the back of the boy's head. They could almost read her lips; 'That will teach you, young man!'

'I might just...' Tom began, as he searched for a clean page in the little leather book. 'You never know, it might be useful — I mean I don't think there are any other roof bosses in here.' And as the stonemason carefully descended the ladder, Tom made a rough sketch of the roof boss above them. The feather quill was adequate, but would only allow for a rudimentary line drawing.

As Tom completed his hurried sketch, he noticed the mason turn and wink at Jack before packing his tools away and wandering off along the walkway. Tom remembered how Bishop Herbert had smiled at Jack earlier and it dawned on him that as Jack seemed familiar with these people, he must have met them before. He decided that it was time to confront their little companion.

'Jack,' he said quietly as the Clock-Jack turned inquisitively towards him, 'How do you know these people? How can they help us?' The Clock-Jack's moustache twitched nervously at one end. 'More to the point Jack, how can *you* help us to get back?' Jack's eyes lit up when he heard this question and his ticking got even louder. He now sounded like a little grandfather clock on legs;

He has been imprisoned for such a long time,
I need you to find a dear friend of mine.
As for me I will help where I can and I must,
for I am a companion in whom you can trust!

'Yeah, a companion of sorts,' whispered Tom under his breath, remembering what Nathaniel Rowbottom had written in the book. 'Anyway, that's not a straight answer. What do you mean he has been imprisoned? Who has been imprisoned and when? What's it got to do with us? I don't even know what year we are in!'

The Clock-Jack said nothing.

'Jack!!'

Tom gripped the antique book more tightly in the frustrating, uncooperative silence. If Jack wouldn't help them, then maybe the book would, if only he studied it more closely. He resolved to do just that as he followed Emma, trudging off along the Cloister towards the Cathedral. Suddenly, Jack turned to face them:

Would you like to see a face that you know?
A monk, Brother Nicholas, from so long ago!

This was such a strange question that Tom stopped dead in his tracks. He didn't have a brother called Nicholas. In fact he didn't have a brother at all. Trying to work out Jack's rhyme, they turned a corner and came face to face with Mr Nicholas, their history teacher from school. For a moment Tom and Emma stood there in stunned silence, both staring incredulously at the figure before them.

What the...Who...How did you...?' Tom's mind was racing. How could this be Mr Nicholas, standing there directly in front of them? It made no sense at all. As he was grappling with this, Tom slowly began to notice that on closer inspection, the figure in front of them didn't look exactly the same as the Mr Nicholas they knew. As he studied the man more carefully, Tom saw that his nose was slightly more crooked and that he had a lot less hair than Mr Nicholas. Also, the figure stood before them was dressed from head to toe in black woollen robes which Tom guessed meant that this man was a monk. One thing was sure; Mr Nicholas was a history teacher and not a monk at this or any other Cathedral.

Whilst these thoughts were swirling around his head, the monk in front of them bowed and said in a soft, kind voice, 'Hello Tom, hello Emma,' and turning to the little Clock-Jack, added 'and good morning to you Jack. It's nice to have you with us once again.' He waited for a moment and then added, 'I've been waiting for you.'

'How do you know our names and why have you been waiting for us? Emma demanded. Tom was taken aback by her forthrightness.

'My name is Brother Nicholas' he continued, ignoring her question, 'for we are all brothers here in God's great family.'

As he said this several more monks emerged from a doorway and came over to join them. They were wearing the same black woollen clothes as Brother Nicholas. Tom noticed that they each had a leather belt tied around the waist and thought that he could see sandals on the monks' feet, although their long black cloaks made it difficult to tell. Some of their robes were dirty with stains and old bits of food. The group certainly did not share Brother Nicholas' apparent soft approach and were a decidedly rough looking bunch. They pushed, shoved and jostled their way over. 'Huh! Children again – I don't know why we bother,' huffed a particularly large monk at the front of the group. 'On some daft rescue mission again I suspect. Trying to get him out of prison. It never works – never has and never will!'

'Rescue mission...?' stuttered Emma.

'True, Brother Michael,' interrupted another as he bumped into Tom, 'we've got better things to do than to waste our time here!'

Brother Nicholas sensed

trouble and stepped between the children and the abrasive monks. 'Welcome to your great adventure,' he said in a hurry and then added rather ominously, 'let us hope you are more successful than our last traveller. Come, we shall walk for a while around the Cloister.'

At that, all the monks bowed somewhat grudgingly towards their guests, with a great deal of tutting and whispering. They then walked slowly away in a rather chaotic procession. Jack motioned for the children to follow and they hurried to catch up.

'I don't blame you for being confused and unsure as to what is happening to you,' said Brother Nicholas calmly, once he was sure that the other monks were out of earshot. 'I'm sure it can be very disorientating at first. But let me reassure you that I am here to help you on your way as safely and as speedily as possible.'

'But why are we here,' pleaded Emma.

'All in good time,' came the rather unsatisfying response. 'Let us familiarise ourselves with our surroundings first.'

Before Emma could open her mouth to reply, Brother Nicholas pointed to the wall on the left. 'Here are the book cupboards,' he motioned, 'in which we store our Bibles and other holy books used for worship...and here,' he nodded to the stone benches that flanked the length of each walkway, 'is where we play games!' Tom was surprised when he heard this — he thought the monks they had just met didn't seem a particularly fun bunch, not the sort to be into playing games.

They were invited to sit down on one of the stone benches. In a second the other monks had reappeared and gathered round, jostling and pushing in rather too closely for comfort. 'Now

Emma,' Brother Nicholas quizzed, 'can you complete our little game?' She looked down to where the monk was pointing and saw nine small round circles cut into the stone bench. 'Nine Men's Morris,' said Brother Nicholas — 'perhaps you know what to do?'

'Pooh!' said a gruff voice from the back, 'As if she would know. I'm certainly not going to help!' Ignoring this rudeness she studied the bench carefully. Some of the cut circles on the bench had been filled with small rounded pieces of stone but some spaces were still empty. Two golden yellow stones had been placed next to one another. She was struggling. 'I'm not sure what to do,' she said, turning to Tom for help. As she did so, Tom noticed her touch the silver locket around her neck, the locket that contained the miniature pictures of their father and mother. He knew that she was drawing inspiration from something deeper and more powerful than any of the monks could have imagined. It was comforting for him too.

He thought for a moment and then handed Emma the small leather book. 'Here,' he said, 'it might contain a clue.' It took her a minute or so to find the right page. Amongst hurried drawings of the Nine Men's Morris board was written the words:

Remember the gemstones
You have in your pocket
For the monks' unusual puzzle
They will help you unlock it - NR

Emma blinked and stared at the page for a moment longer. And then it dawned on her.

'Yes!' she shouted, 'the gemstones I bought in the antique shop earlier today,' and then hastily corrected herself, 'or whenever it was.' If she could find them now, one of the stones might fit into the empty space and she would complete the game. She rummaged in her pockets and sure enough right there were the smooth and shining stones. She placed them on the stone bench and saw that one, a beautiful golden yellow stone, fitted perfectly into the empty space. Triumphantly, she placed the gemstone into the puzzle to make a line of three golden stones. Brother Nicholas clapped in applause. One or two of the other monks begrudgingly did the same, but their lack of response didn't stop Emma from bursting out in to a wide grin.

'Well done!' exclaimed Brother Nicholas as he got to his feet. 'You know we're often allowed to play this game out in the Cloister. Brother Peter here is our champion.' Brother Peter pushed to the front and forced a smile through gritted teeth. 'Huh — beginners luck I'd say. I could beat you at Nine Men's Morris any day.'

'Yeah…?' replied Tom.

Brother Nicholas shot the monk a reproachful glance. 'Well, yes, thank you for that Brother Peter, now back to your work in the kitchens I think.'

As the crowd began to disperse once again, Brother Nicholas seemed to become agitated. His face clouded over and he nodded silently for a moment, musing to himself. 'Remember the number nine Emma,' he warned, with a serious and foreboding voice.

'Remember it well – for the serpents will demand a verse from you and will not let you pass without it.' On saying this he motioned for them to follow as he moved quickly away.

As they hurried after him, Tom nudged Emma and she gave him back the small green leather book. 'Nine Men's Morris,' he said to himself. He removed the feather quill and quickly scribbled the number nine down on to a clean, fresh page.

9

Tom had no idea how it might help them, but Brother Nicholas had obviously told them something of much importance. As far as he could tell, no other numbers had been written in the book – perhaps Nathaniel had not completed the game of Nine Men's Morris and had never been given this clue. And then it dawned on Tom that perhaps the number nine wasn't a clue at all and would in fact do them no good whatsoever. How did they know what was right and what was wrong? How could they be sure who to trust? Most of the other monks had so far been as unhelpful as possible.

As he rejoined the rest of the group, Tom overheard one of the monks explaining why they were all living at the Cathedral and what they did every day. 'Eight times a day we are in the Cathedral worshipping,' he said '...and at other times we are working.'

'What kind of work do you do?' panted Tom, trying to take his mind off serpents and whether or not the number nine was a clue to the verse they needed. 'Many kinds!' exclaimed the monk, impatience showing in his voice. 'We take great care looking after the sick and the poor who come to us for help. Or we may be out working in the fields or in the herb garden. Often we sit out here in the Cloister reading, writing and making copies of holy books. It takes dedication to become a monk you know! I don't expect you to understand,' he finished, shooting Tom a snooty glance.

'They really are a friendly bunch…' Tom muttered so that only Emma could here.

Brother Nicholas proceeded to point out many of the rooms used by the monks, all of which led off from the Cloister walkways. As far as Tom could make out, the monks had a meeting room, a dormitory (which was a kind of communal bedroom), a hospital, a dining room and a guest hall. He also heard Brother Nicholas say that there was a special room in which the monks could talk to one another. Tom thought this was strange. 'Surely you are allowed to talk to one another whenever you like?' he asked.

'Not quite,' boomed a monk right behind him in a deep, threatening voice, causing Tom to jump. 'We live by very strict rules here you know which are all written down in a book. These tell us what we can and can't do; what we can eat, what we can wear, how we should behave and how we should organise our time. The rules were written down by a man called Benedict and because we follow his rules we are known as Benedictines. It's simple really.' He stopped, sniffed and almost by accident blurted out, 'And if you ask me, I don't see why we have to get ourselves involved with these silly rescue missions!' With that he folded his arms and sat down.

'Yes, thank you Brother Timothy,' interrupted Brother

Nicholas, 'I will explain from here.' He told the children exactly what time the monks woke up, when they worshipped, when they worked and when they ate together. He finished by saying that some of the present group found it difficult to follow these rules exactly. 'Their hospitality to strangers could certainly improve,' he concluded, 'that's for sure.'

Tom found it all quite confusing and so decided to write down what Brother Nicholas was saying. He sat down on one of the long stone benches and rummaged for the book in his jacket pocket. He started to scribble as best he could. Yet before writing down any more of what Brother Nicholas was saying he turned to a fresh, clean page and wrote in large, clear capital letters across it:

RESCUE MISSION?

Chapter Seven

Fire From Heaven

Tom hurriedly finished his note and tucked the book and quill away in his pocket. As he did so, he heard Brother Nicholas say that one of the rules of behaviour in the monastery was that the monks had to spend most of their time in silence. 'We live in a very simple way – as God intended,' said the monk. He turned to Jack; 'Perhaps you can help me explain:'

The monks keep their silence for most of the day
this helps them to focus, to worship and pray;
even at dinner they must not say a word
for the rules are quite clear and must be observed.

This mention of dinner had the effect of making both children instantly hungry and, perhaps noticing their semi-permanent drool, Brother Nicholas suggested they all move to the Refectory for supper. This turned out to be a huge dining hall and was situated on the southern side of the Cloister. It could easily accommodate the entire community of monks within. Tom's heart sank a little as he contemplated the prospect of more hostility from the other monks, but Jack had rhymed that they would all be eating in silence, which for the first time in his life seemed very attractive to Tom.

Supper when it came was simple but nourishing, consisting of eggs, bread, cheese and fruit. The food was washed down by several pints of dark and cloudy ale. Tom gulped it down and it went straight to his head. The food was brought to them by servants — townsfolk perhaps, certainly not monks for they were dressed very differently. Yet they too were silent. There was one voice however, for during the meal all those in the hall listened to a lone monk, perched up high in a gallery. He was reading to them from the Bible.

'The reading is to feed the spirit as well as the body,' Brother Nicholas explained as they left the Refectory some time later. Tom was only half-listening. He was dizzy with the ale and was making a big effort to concentrate on the steps leading back down into the Cloister. He tried to focus on the steps immediately ahead. Yet they all seemed to be moving. It was no surprise then that he failed to see one of them sticking up unevenly in front of him and he tripped, falling flat on his face, hitting the ground with a crumpling thud. A loud belch followed by a ripple of laughter

broke out from the group of monks following behind. Tom tried to ignore them. He felt a stinging pain in his leg and looked down to see blood trickling from just below his knee.

'Oh dear, oh dear,' said Brother Nicholas, hurrying over. 'Whatever have you done?'

'I was...stepping...along...the path

thingy and...'

'Yes and Cathedral ale can be quite potent,' the monk chuckled, realising that Tom was not seriously hurt. 'Come,' he said, 'let us take you to be healed – it is not far to the Infirmary.'

Tom struggled to his feet and managed to hobble a few steps towards a large open doorway. 'The Infirmary is where the sick and poorly monks are taken,' whispered Emma. 'It's a bit like a hospital I suppose. But...' she continued, with a sense of mischief in her voice, 'you'd better beware of the bleeding chamber!' Tom sobered up in an instant.

'The...the bleeding chamber?' he retorted, but before he had time to ask her exactly what went on in there, Brother Nicholas had led them through the doorway and was ushering them into a cool, darkened stone room. Another monk suddenly appeared. 'Ah, Brother Simon, how good to see you. I'm afraid Tom here has had a fall and needs your attention.' Turning to the children he continued with a smile, 'and perhaps something for a forthcoming headache. Brother Simon is our Infirmarer and he is here to make you well. He will prepare medicine for you.' With that he disappeared out through the doorway.

'I hope he's friendlier than the rest of them,' spluttered Tom, not relishing his prospects.

Brother Simon motioned for them to sit down and began his task. He had taken some leaves from a stone jar and was crushing them in a small mixing bowl. He added a little water to this and continued to mix, occasionally looking over to Tom and Emma. The grinding of the leaves in the stone bowl echoed around the room and put Tom on edge. He was starting to sweat. Building up his courage he asked, 'Er...um...Brother Simon..., are you going to take me... (he gulped)...to... the... er...bleeding chamber?' He felt glad that he had managed to ask the question but now feared the monks reply. Brother Simon looked at them in silence, a slight smile breaking at the corners of his mouth. He reached over to the bench and picked up a small, sharp looking surgical knife. He wiped it on his robes and took a few paces towards them. Tom drew himself back to the cold wall behind as the monk raised the knife above his head.

'Oh no, no,' Brother Simon laughed..., 'your cut is only small and can be dealt with here. We have exactly what we need.' He swung the knife in their direction before pointing it around the stone chamber. Tom felt somewhat relieved and was about to ask who actually went into the bleeding chamber and what exactly happened to them in there anyway, when Jack, who had been sitting quietly on the stone bench next to Emma, got to his feet and said quietly:

The monks believe that if your blood turns rotten,
it must be removed and quickly forgotten!

The Clock-Jack sat down and looked hurriedly from Brother Simon to Tom and then back to Brother Simon again. Tom hadn't a clue what Jack had meant by this. How could your blood turn rotten and then be forgotten? 'Yes, well,' began the Infirmarer, coughing slightly as he spoke, 'we believe that sickness is sometimes caused by bad blood in the body and so to remain well, the bad blood has to be removed. It is, um, how shall I put it, drained away.'

Tom looked at Emma who turned to the monk and said, 'How exactly do you remove the bad blood, Brother?'

'Ah, we are perfecting that art,' the monk replied, swishing the small knife in an arc above his head. 'But rest assured, we are taking great care and consideration – I usually practice on pigs you know.' Tom felt faint. The thought of being cut open to allow some of his blood to be drained away in order to help him get better was one of the silliest things he'd heard. It was a very, very strange idea indeed. Surely doing that would make the patient feel worse?

Just as he was about to put that thought to Brother Simon, the monk came over and sat down beside him. 'Now swallow this,' he said, passing the bowl to Tom. 'The leaves of woad will help to stem the flow of blood, but your head may swim even more afterwards!' Tom gulped the mixture down quickly. It certainly wasn't the best thing he had ever tasted, but on balance he was sure that this was better than being taken to the bleeding chamber and sliced open. 'When the woad begins to work, I shall need to apply root of madder to the wound,' said Brother Simon, smiling. 'Thank you,' replied Tom, rather pathetically – he had no idea what this mad monk was talking about. He lay down and gritted his teeth.

∞

By the time they found Brother Nicholas again in the Cloister, the sky had darkened over and it looked as if a storm was about to break.

Save for the friendly monk, the Cloister was deserted and desolate. The children looked up to see swirls of grey and black cloud gathering thunderously over the Cathedral. The air had turned cold and the wind was beginning to moan its way around the building. Tom saw the wooden Spire reaching up high above them, almost into the heavens it seemed, and thought how vulnerable it looked against the blackening sky. It seemed to creak with fear as the wind gathered pace and whipped around it.

'Good, you are healed. Now follow me quickly,' shouted Brother Nicholas as a worried look broke across his face. 'Fire from heaven - there will be fire from heaven! Hurry!' At this, a gigantic crack of thunder burst and echoed around the Cloister, filling the walkways with a sharp ear-splitting roar. The children both jumped with fright at the sound. They had heard a bang like that before, when standing in the sitting room of the river gatehouse with Mr Postwick. Jack was looking extremely nervous too andsang hurriedly:

The great storm is coming and fire from the sky
dancing and crashing, exploding on high;
let us take shelter for now is the time
for Jack to be silent and finish his rhyme.

He then doffed his hat to them and sprinted off along the walkway. As he watched, Tom thought momentarily how odd the Clock-Jack looked with his little legs rotating like a propeller as he zoomed away. 'Hurry,' said Brother Nicholas with fear in his voice. 'Let us follow – quickly!' As they scrambled away, another crack of thunder erupted around them and this time it was followed by a fierce flash of lightning that lit up the gathering gloom. 'Fire from heaven,' cried Brother Nicholas again as the lightning crackled and fizzed all around them. Rain started to pour down as yet another finger of lightning streaked across the night sky.

Emma turned to see another bolt of lightning narrowly miss the tall wooden Spire. A fourth stream of white light jolted from the darkness and this time the Spire was not so fortunate. In a second, the lightning had connected with the fragile wooden structure which in turn exploded in a shower of sparks and light. The children watched open-mouthed as the Spire erupted into flames and came toppling down before them. For a heart stopping moment it seemed as if they would all be crushed under its weight. Yet it collapsed and fell on to the Cathedral itself, shattering the wooden roof in a roaring sea of fire, sparks and burning debris. It was impossible to describe the terror of the noise as the Spire came crashing down.

As they stood there transfixed, a great wave of heat swept over them, singeing their hair and clothes and almost knocking them off their feet. Stay here any longer and they would be burnt to a crisp. Brother Nicholas swooped to pick them up and, carrying one child under each arm, he flew out of the Cloister, heading in the direction of the river. As the monk set them down, Tom had time to turn and see the great building on fire. It was a terrifying and yet magnificent sight as the crackling and hissing flames devoured the wooden roof which gave way quickly and crashed onto the Cathedral floor below.

By now the whole structure was engulfed in flames and huge plumes of smoke were trailing upwards. Tom wondered if this destruction could ever be repaired as the smoke streamed from the stricken building. His heart leapt in hope — perhaps the three serpents would be devoured in the flames too and they might not, after all, have to confront them. Such thoughts occupied his mind as they battled towards the safety of the river.

Chapter Eight

The Missing Map

The little group slept by the river for some time following their escape from the great fire. The silence was complete.

Brother Nicholas was the first to stir and wake. He quietly wandered off to the apple orchard in order to collect a much welcome breakfast. The ordeal had been such that when they awoke, they recovered in silence, munching hungrily away on the fruit. The only other sound was Jack's mechanical, rhythmic ticking. It was peculiar to hear and it served as a reminder that time was marching inexorably onwards. It also jolted Tom into realising that they seemed no nearer to discovering the verse with which they might have to confront the serpents.

When he felt the moment was right, Brother Nicholas began to explain all that had happened to them. 'The new stone Cloister was completed by the year 1450 — you saw a stonemason completing one of his carvings I think. Only thirteen years later the fire came down from heaven.' He paused, as if contemplating the destructive fury of the storm they had just witnessed. 'Soon after, a magnificent new roof and Spire were rebuilt in stone — essential to prevent them from catching fire again! In the new roof of the Cathedral, hundreds of roof bosses were added to tell the story of the Bible.' Tom's spirits lifted a little when he heard that the Pharaoh drowning in the Red Sea was one of these new roof bosses. Perhaps they might have a chance to see it after all.

Emma had been silent and still up until this moment, but their conversation prompted her into life. 'So we've jumped through time again,' she muttered and then turning to Jack added 'or ticked through it. So far we have gone from the building of the Cathedral in 1096 to the great fire of, let me see...1450 plus thirteen...1463!' She half-heartedly tapped her watch. It was still stuck at seven minutes past seven. 'But where will we be taken to next?' she began to sob, 'and how will we get home?'

At this, Brother Nicholas took pity on her and moved to put a comforting arm around her shoulders. 'Travellers all must return to their own time through the north door of the Cathedral — but that much you know already,' he said softly. 'That is the only true route, but it is difficult and dangerous. The door is guarded by three terrible serpents.' He paused for a moment to find the right choice of words. 'The serpents will devour without mercy any unprepared traveller who attempts to pass below them. Many have fallen victim to their evil.'

The monk stopped and looked contemplatively across the river. It was as if a powerful memory had troubled him. 'Nathaniel was a dear friend of mine,' he mused bitterly, 'a man of much courage and wisdom. He, like many others, fell prey to the serpents' fangs.'

Tom had opened the antique book and was studying it carefully. This was the first real opportunity that he had had to have a good look through it. They appeared to be in no immediate danger, they were resting and it was broad daylight. As he was leafing through, it became clear that Nathaniel Rowbottom had not been the only previous owner. Next to a particularly fine sketch of the new stone Spire was scribbled:

the spire, after the great fire of 1463 ~ by Osberto Reynolds
time traveller and antiquary

'That's right,' said Brother Nicholas, glancing towards Tom. 'The book has been owned by many before you — and will be found by many after you as well.'

'I'm not going to lose it,' stated Tom defiantly.

Brother Nicholas smiled. 'It will help you — but only up to a point,' he said. 'To pass safely through the north door and return to your father you must recite a verse to the serpents. They have already chosen for you what that verse must be. Each traveller is set a different verse — you see the serpents are cunning and do not want travellers to pass the same verse onto one another!

The children listened intently as he continued more quietly. 'Yet the serpents cannot prevent the book from passing between time travellers and some of the clues left by our forebears may be of assistance. Still, be mindful on your journey with Jack here to collect the clues that will point you to the verse the serpents have chosen as yours. It will always be a verse related to you, personal and connected to your thoughts, feelings and desires.'

By now, Brother Nicholas' voice had become barely a whisper and the children had to move very close in order to hear him. 'Be on your guard, mind, for the serpents have great power. They are able, at times, to possess those whom you may see as friends.' He paused and then continued in a voice that was barely audible. 'You must give the serpents your verse at precisely the right moment and only then can you return. Yet you will face them regardless of whether you have the verse or not – the ticking of our little friend here is a reminder to you that time is slipping away and your confrontation draws ever closer.'

The children sat in thoughtful silence contemplating what Brother Nicholas had told them. Tom frowned as he studied the book again for clues, yet it still made little sense. On one page, four names had been written and then three had been crossed through with a line:

Matthew Mark
Luke John

Perhaps this was a clue to pay particular attention to anyone they might meet called Mark, as his was the only name with no line through it. Or then again perhaps it was nothing of the sort.

'There is something else though, isn't there?' said Emma bluntly, standing and brushing the hair from her face. 'The monk, I mean one of the rude ones in the Cloister...he said something about us being on a rescue mission. And Mr Postwick mumbled on about rescuing someone as well.'

Jack sat bolt upright at the mention of the Gatekeeper's name. 'What did they both mean?'

Brother Nicholas turned away, not wanting to catch her eye.

'The City of Light...' he whispered to himself, as if the words were not meant to be spoken. 'Could it be that these two children can achieve it? No, that is impossible for me to tell.....I am sorry.' He gestured towards Tom who passed him the small leather book. The monk opened it to where the centre pages should have been. 'These pages have been missing for as long as anyone can remember,' he began, 'but it is thought that the map that was once drawn upon them reveals the truth.'

'The truth?' repeated Tom.

'The truth of where he is imprisoned,' answered Brother Nicholas coldly, 'of how he can be rescued and...of how the City of Light will be created.'

The children were motionless and hanging on the monk's every word.

'Of where who is and...and...and what is a City of Light?' started Emma. But the monk interrupted. 'There are forces beyond our control that have sent you here on his behalf. Yet without this map', he gestured to the missing centre pages, 'it is almost impossible for you to succeed.' He paused in silent reflection. 'The only course open for you is to return as quickly and as safely as possible and to try and retrieve the map from somewhere near your starting point. Somewhere near the river gatehouse I should imagine.'

Tom was gazing out across the river and only half-listening. 'So no-one has succeeded before,' he whispered to himself. 'That's why we're here.'

'Exactly who is this person to be rescued anyway?' said Emma forcefully, oblivious to her brother and desperate to ask the question.

Brother Nicholas looked at her and clenched his jaw. He would have no more of it. Pulling himself up and reaching out his hands he said, 'Come, let us return to the Cathedral — we need to lift our spirits.'

Chapter Nine

The Angel

On re-entering the great building, they were met by a wall of noise — and a cascade of colour and light that momentarily swept aside their doubts and uncertainties. Huge, colourful flags and banners were draped from the galleries and upper levels; the arches, columns and windows shimmered with decorative paintings and designs. The small group made its way towards the noise — into the Nave of the Cathedral, the huge open space where the people of the City came in to worship. Tom looked up to the ceiling, repaired as Brother Nicholas had told them, following the great fire of 1463. It was now complete with all its marvellously carved roof bosses. He looked hard to find his favourite and sure enough, above the altar table and silver cross, he saw the carving of the Egyptian Pharaoh drowning in the Red Sea.

He thought how stunning the Cathedral looked with thousands of flowers strewn across the stone floor and the many candles spreading light into every corner. Emma too marvelled at the beautiful pictures and stories illuminated in the great stained glass windows and couldn't help but whisper a 'wow' to no one in particular. It was a warm and welcome distraction from their recent conversation at the river.

There were many hundreds of people inside the Cathedral, all jostling for position in an attempt to get as close as possible to the altar table at the front. Tom felt worried that Jack, who was after all only about a metre tall, might get lost in the crowd. But their travelling companion seemed to be having the time of his life, waving and smiling at many of the people in the crowd. Suddenly, everyone fell silent and turned as one to face the great west doors. As they did so, the organ behind them burst into noise. It sounded like a hundred trumpets playing all at once as the children also turned to face westwards.

Coming through the doors was a long procession of monks, some dressed in fine, brightly coloured cloaks and others in their usual black. They had been transformed from the rough and tumble group that the children had first met in the Cloister. They were calm and well behaved – and by the looks of it, revelling in the attention they were receiving. Tom smiled as he recognised Brother Simon, the Infirmarer, near the front of the procession. The monk mouthed silently to Tom. 'How's the knee?' and Tom nodded his head in return, putting both thumbs in the air. Brother Simon beamed at this as he headed away towards the altar.

The monks started to sing as they moved around the building and after a little while all the people joined in to make one great wave of noise. With the organ playing, many bells ringing and the multitude of voices, it was a magical scene and it struck Tom that it must be an occasion of great importance. 'Today is Corpus Christi,' explained Brother Nicholas, 'when we celebrate the sharing of bread and wine. Our Lord of course shared bread and wine with his disciples during the Last Supper.' All around, the scene was certainly one of great joy and celebration. The children felt happy and safe to be there with all these people.

'No serpent could get at us here,' shouted Tom to his sister above the noise. Brother Nicholas interrupted, 'Let us join the procession for there is much more to see.' With this the two children, together with Jack, followed Brother Nicholas as he scurried after the last of the monks. They were processing underneath the organ, leaving the mass of people behind them in the Nave. In front of them lay carved wooden benches, flanking upwards to both left and right. This was the Choir, and behind the benches were beautifully carved wooden seats with elaborate canopies above. There were trees, leaves, branches and birds of prey carved delicately into the wood.

'Look,' Emma shouted, 'the tiny wooden heads!' Tom turned to the right and his heart leapt. Just above him were some peculiarly carved human faces, each set perfectly into the wooden canopy. Each was very small and each of the mouths was poking its tongue out. It was an odd sight. 'Why on earth are they doing that?' he asked.

'No reason in particular,' smiled Brother Nicholas, 'perhaps the wood carver was having a bit of fun!' He brought them to a stop, leaving the monks to carry on ahead. The procession continued until it was out of sight, but the monks' singing could still be heard echoing all around the Cathedral. He led them over to a row of fine wooden seats and sat down on the first one he came to. 'Ah, that's better,' he sighed. 'We older monks need as much rest as we can get!'

He placed his elbows on the delicately carved arm rests and explained that the whole seat could in fact be tipped upwards. 'By resting on the ledges of the upturned seats we gain some comfort from our long hours of worship,' he said, leaning forward to reveal an intricately carved picture underneath. It was another peculiar head and seemed to have leaves and branches shooting out from its mouth and then encircling it. 'The Green Man,' breezed Brother Nicholas — 'an ancient and mysterious symbol of new life and resurrection.'

'If I were a monk,' Tom chipped in, 'I wouldn't want to stand up all the time, so these seats would be pretty useful.'

'They have a special name,' chimed Brother Nicholas. 'They are called misericords, which means mercy seats.' Tom thought he ought to write that name down in the antique book as it might be of use. Yet he decided against it. After all, it was a very tricky spelling.

Hoping that he wouldn't regret that later, he looked across to Jack whom he expected might pipe up at this point to explain further. Yet the Clock-Jack was busy in thought as he carefully inspected the reading stand that stood tall and proud in the centre of the misericords.

They wandered over to the stand which looked very much like a magnificent golden eagle. 'This lectern has been carved into the shape of a pelican,' exclaimed Brother Nicholas proudly, 'and stands in the centre of the Crossing.'

In the area immediately in front of them, Tom recognised the stone Cathedra upon which they had seen Bishop Herbert de Losinga sitting. He felt a pang of doubt once again.

Emma was struggling to work out how the carved bird in front of them could possibly be a pelican when it so obviously looked like an eagle. 'Brother Nicholas,' started Emma, 'that looks nothing like a pelican, how can it...'

'Ah', interrupted the monk quickly, 'just as with the roof bosses, it is unlikely that the craftsman here had ever seen a real pelican. So he did his best to guess!' He thought for a moment, 'perhaps travellers to far and distant lands told him stories of these strange birds...actually I'm not really sure.'

Tom was shocked to hear Brother Nicholas unable to fully explain. 'Why did it have to be a pelican,' he asked, before wishing that he'd kept his mouth shut.

'That I do know,' smiled the monk — 'it's an old story, a legend really. If Pelicans were unable to find food for their young, they would return to the nest and feed them with blood. You see the mother Pelican here would peck at its own chest and...well it's a symbolic story connected to...'

'Urggghh,' said Tom interupting. 'Sounds disgusting. Look, you can see where it's tapping away at its chest. You can see the blood trickling down!'

'Does a Pelican really do that?' asked Emma, inspecting the Pelican closely.

'As I said, it's more of a symbolic story,' Brother Nicholas replied. 'It's...' Yet he got no further for at that moment Jack jumped off his misericord, cleared his throat and announced:

Time to return to the Cathedral Nave floor
for a sight to see like never before;
an angel and incense and smoke all around
let us be quick and join the great sound.

Brother Nicholas shrugged. In no time at all the four of them were back in the Cathedral Nave amongst the huge crowd of people gathered there to worship. There was much rejoicing with singing, music and the jingling of bells. 'It must be near the end,' said Tom, motioning to where the monks were leaving through the open west doors. Jack led them to the centre of the Nave and shouted above the great din:

Look up and you'll see a marvellous sight,
a magnificent angel swooping in flight!

As Jack was finishing these words the whole crowd fell silent, looking upwards towards the wonderfully decorated ceiling. In the centre was a hole, something which they had not noticed before. It looked unusual – almost as if one of the roof bosses had come crashing down. Or maybe a mistake had been made and the stonemasons had left a gap. Tom thought this was highly unlikely though, considering how skilled and careful they seemed to be. There was no way in the world he could have imagined what was about to happen next. The crowd gasped in delight as very slowly and very carefully the figure of a beautifully carved and painted wooden angel was lowered through the hole. It looked to be suspended on ropes or perhaps chains as it was lowered towards them. Tom saw that it held a rounded silver casket in its hands. 'There must be someone above the ceiling,' exclaimed Emma, 'gently lowering the angel towards us!'

They were mesmerised by the sight — having never seen anything like it before. The angel came to rest just above their heads and began to swing round and round. This made it seem as if it was flying and Tom noticed that this also caused wisps of white smoke to escape from the casket. As the smoke began to fill the Cathedral the air became warm and sweet smelling. He had smelt incense in a church before but nothing as strong or as powerful as this. The people around them were just as excited and amazed as great shouts of joy and praise erupted around the building.

Both Tom and Emma were captivated by all that was happening — it really was a breathtaking scene. With the angel flying around above them and the accompanying smiles and shouts of joy, their hearts were at last lifted and they were intoxicated by feelings of hope and happiness.

Chapter Ten

In The Clouds

The crowds at the Corpus Christi service eventually cleared to leave Tom, Emma, Jack and Brother Nicholas standing alone in the centre of the Nave. The children were disappointed to see the mass of people disappear and the noise, colour and sheer spectacle of the service come to an end. Brother Nicholas could sense this, so he turned to look at the little Clock-Jack, who responded immediately:

Perhaps you would like to climb up the Spire?
To do it you must travel higher and higher!

Emma's face lit up at the prospect of climbing the Spire and she instantly forgot her disappointment. 'But how can we?' Tom whispered under his breath to her. 'The wooden spire was destroyed by that great lightning strike. We saw it with our very own eyes.' Brother Nicholas turned to look at Jack again who winked and smiled:

The great Bishop Goldwell had built our new Spire
not twenty years after the disastrous fire;
but now it's constructed in stone so grand
so it's one of the tallest in all of the land!

'So if Bishop Goldwell had the stone Spire built twenty or so years after the fire,' murmured Emma, quickly doing her maths, 'and bearing in mind how long it might have taken to build...er...we must be roughly in the year, um let's see...about 1500!'

'There or thereabouts,' smiled Brother Nicholas, beckoning for them to follow. Tom looked back into the little antique leather book, for he had suddenly remembered the sketch of the new Spire by Osberto Reynolds.

As he looked at the picture, Tom wondered whether Brother Nicholas had invited Osberto to climb the Spire on some previous adventure. Perhaps this had given Osberto false hope in his failed mission to collect the verse that was to be personal to him.

Nevertheless, the prospect of climbing the Spire was thrilling and Tom wondered how far they would be able to see when they reached the top. He followed the others through a doorway to be confronted by a steep spiral staircase that twisted away to the right. As he started to climb he could hear Emma deep in conversation with Brother Nicholas. She was asking him all sorts of questions about the Cathedral, its history and how the building was used. Tom knew that she was digging for information that would help them. Who was imprisoned, how might they find him and what good would it do them? He willed her to ask the monk about the mysterious City of Light. But for some reason, Brother Nicholas was giving very little away. He did overhear something about the monks often walking in procession around these upper levels and half expected to bump into Brother Simon and all the others singing and chanting as they went.

Tom made a determined effort to catch up with them and it seemed, just for a moment, as if Brother Nicholas was waiting for him to do so. 'So how long have you been a monk?' he heard Emma ask. 'Oh...for many, many years now,' replied Brother Nicholas. 'In fact I am one of the oldest and longest serving monks here.' He stopped and turned to look at them both. 'My time now grows short. Yet remember,' he said clearly, 'to always watch *your* time.'

'And add it to nine,' mumbled Jack, as he bit one of his tiny fingernails and looked away.

'Ha! That's right,' chuckled the monk. 'Watch your time and add it to nine!!'

He turned and continued on his way up the spiral staircase. 'Wait, what do you mean?' Tom blurted out after him, scrambling around the spiral steps. 'Add what to nine? Brother Nicholas, wait!' But the monk had gone, his footsteps echoing from the stone walls as he made his ascent.

The stone staircases eventually gave way to

a series of rough wooden ladders and it became darker and darker the higher they climbed. Tom was lost in thought, trying to figure out the meaning of what Brother Nicholas and Jack had just said. 'Watch your time...and add it to nine,' he repeated. Why did they have to wrap things in riddles? Why couldn't the monk and Clock-Jack just be straight with them and give them the clues they needed? Surely Brother Nicholas wanted them to find their way safely home? These thoughts distracted Tom because he didn't notice that the others had come to a halt. He continued on his own thoughtful way to the top of one of the ladders until he bumped heavily into Jack, who being rather small and lightweight almost toppled over with a grumpy huff and puff.

Tom could have sworn that he heard a hiss as the little Clock-Jack got back to his feet. He was about to whisper this to Emma when Brother Nicholas boomed 'Almost there,' from up ahead, followed by 'this is the last ladder!' They hauled themselves up the final few rungs until they stood on a tiny wooden platform, barely big enough to hold the four of them. They were at the very top of the Spire, at its narrowest point and with the cold stone of the structure itself pressing heavily on to their backs. 'Now turn around,' said Brother Nicholas, 'and see!' Very carefully Tom and Emma turned around to face outwards.

'Wow!' they both uttered together. The sky was a clear, deep blue and virtually cloudless. They could see for miles around them – to the immediate surroundings of the Cathedral itself, to the City of Norwich and to the countryside far beyond. They saw that attached to the Cathedral and Cloister were many grand stone and flint buildings with fine red tiled roofs. Not too far away was the River Wensum and Tom's heart leapt as he recognised the river gatehouse at Pull's Ferry. It was the first time they had seen it since leaving their father. Yet Tom doubted whether his Dad was actually asleep inside this particular gatehouse that he could see now. He noticed that a canal had been dug from there towards the Cathedral and remembered seeing all the activity as the stone was unloaded from the huge wooden cargo boats. The boats had sailed right in so as to get as close as possible to the Cathedral building site. Their Dad had been right all along about Pull's Ferry and the canal.

'What are all these buildings for?' Emma asked, realising that on their journey so far, they had been largely confined to the Cathedral itself. 'Well,' replied Brother Nicholas, 'the monastery has many functions and it must have many buildings to serve its needs. Within these buildings we can produce almost everything we need to live. We have offices,' he continued, 'houses, workshops, a bakery, brewery and stores that support our everyday needs.'

'So you never need to go out shopping or anything like that?' she continued. 'No, no,' chuckled Brother Nicholas, 'in fact many people come to us seeking shelter and food. It is our duty to care for the sick, the needy and the forsaken.' Brother Nicholas gazed out lovingly at the buildings surrounding the Cathedral.

As they continued to stare in wonder from their vantage point, Tom rummaged for the leather book and quill and found that the quill's ink was still fresh. 'Amazing,' he whispered under his breath. He had decided to contribute another of his own sketches to the book. Whether or not it would help them or anyone else later he didn't know, but Tom felt that he wanted to record something of what the monk was showing them. It was impossible to sketch everything; there were far too many buildings for that. So he chose one — the river gatehouse at Pull's Ferry.

He worked as quickly as he could for the sky was rapidly clouding over, so much so that some of the buildings were disappearing from view. As he continued hurriedly, Tom sensed that Jack was becoming agitated beside him. He finished quickly and added to his sketch:

Pull's Ferry by Tom Buxton
Time Traveller & school boy

Sketching the gatehouse had reminded Tom of just how much he was missing his father. As he paused, he remembered the way his dad had puzzled over the rickety old pub sign creaking above Pull's Ferry. 'The Knights of the Window,' Tom repeated, his voice trembling a little.

He turned towards Jack, whose ticking seemed to have become even louder and impatient, if such a thing was possible. Perhaps he wanted to return to the ground, Tom thought. As he finished and was returning the book to his pocket, he stole a look at the picture engraved on its front cover. He was sure that he had seen a peculiar flash of green momentarily appear and then vanish somewhere upon it. Tom's eyes focussed on the three unusual heads that were carved into the stonework above the strong and impressive looking door. When he had first found the book, he had been unable to tell who these mysterious heads belonged to. But as he studied them now more carefully the eyes on the central head shone bright green and then faded. And as they did so, Jack hissed venomously at him.

'The three serpents!' Tom screamed and threw the book down on to the floor. Emma spun round to see him cover his face with his hands and Brother Nicholas bend down quickly to recover the book. Jack looked nervously at the monk who shot him a reproachful glance. 'Tom... Tom, be calm, please be calm,' the monk pleaded, 'it is not our little friend Jack here who is to blame. Please do not be angry with him. You see, the serpents are powerful and can possess the unwary. I have already warned you of this.'

Jack's eyes had started to well up with tears as he realised that the serpents had spoken through him. Emma bent down to reassure him and the little Clock-Jack burst into tears on her shoulder. Brother Nicholas drew them all in towards him. 'Listen my dear friends,' he said anxiously, 'for the hands of time are against us.' Tom struggled to regain his composure. 'The serpents are foolish in their bid to divide you,' he continued, 'for they have made a grave mistake.' He held the book above his head. 'You see now the north door itself and the three guardians above. It is clear what you must look for to find your way home. They have unknowingly helped you on your way.'

Whilst the monk had been talking, wisps of cloud had begun to drift in through the wooden slats on the windows and now began to curl and shroud around them all in a foggy haze. 'Come,' said the monk, 'let us hurry back to the ground.'

Jack led the little procession quickly downwards, first descending the rough wooden ladders and then the more impressive and sturdy spiral staircases. Emma and Tom followed, with Brother Nicholas at the rear. Their footsteps echoed loudly, with the noise bouncing around the solid stone walls. The children were deep in whispered conversation.

'Are you okay?' asked Emma, 'that was quite a shock.'
Tom didn't answer. It was clear that he didn't want to talk about it.

'What will happen if we find the north door but don't have the verse,' worried Emma, moving away from what had just happened to them.

'The...the same that has happened to all the others I suppose — we won't make it,' Tom replied, struggling a little. But we can't worry about that now. 'We have to concentrate on finding the clues and recording them in this book.'

'So how many do we have already?'

'I'm not sure. One, possibly two — it's difficult to say.'

The conversation distracted them for a time. When Tom

concentrated once more on descending the stairs, he became acutely aware that no footsteps were following. He stopped, turned and waited. There was nothing – only silence. Brother Nicholas was nowhere to be seen. He had vanished completely. Tom leant against the wall, dizzy and unsure. As he did so, a cold air came swirling around the staircase and with it sighed a ghostly breath; 'Goodbye Tom, goodbye Emma; may God go with you.' He spun round full circle, but there was definitely no-one there.

Standing just ahead, but looking as unhappy as they had ever seen him was Jack. Tom struggled to understand what had happened – why and how had the monk disappeared? He turned to Jack for comfort but the sad little Clock-Jack could only mutter:

The monks are all gone and so is our Brother
and after them now there will be no other;
we are now all alone, but must carry on
for the serpents await and you must be gone

He looked at them with big sullen eyes. Tom remembered meeting Brother Nicholas for the first time – when he had thought that the monk was in fact their history teacher, Mr Nicholas, from school. He'd had a strange thought enter his head then and had wondered if it was possible that Brother Nicholas was actually a distant ancestor of their history teacher. Anything was possible and there was a resemblance. He puffed up his cheeks and let out a long sigh – the emotion of the last few minutes and this latest experience had exhausted him. He turned to Emma and knew that she too needed a rest. Yet Jack would have none of it and insisted that they continue their descent from the Spire. They reluctantly agreed and so began once more.

As Tom recovered from the shock of losing Brother Nicholas he thought about what the monk had said at the top of the Spire. Had the serpents really made a mistake in showing them the doorway through which they must travel? Or were the serpents trying to entice them into their lair in order that they were easier prey? Had they also possessed Brother Nicholas during his last few minutes with them? These were troubling questions as the spiral stone staircases finally gave way to the floor of the Cathedral.

Chapter Eleven

The Smiling Skeleton

They were in a despondent mood as they finally reached the Cathedral floor. It rapidly became clear that the Cathedral they returned too had changed dramatically. It was as if the disappearance of the monk had somehow caused an alteration in the way the Cathedral looked. Initially, the building seemed to be in a good state of repair and looked as if it was certainly still used as a place of worship. But it was, somehow, different.

Tom immediately saw a large number of books collected near the stone pulpit. He walked over and picked one of them up. 'Emma, look,' he shouted, 'this Bible is brand new.' Sure enough the Bible in his hands was shiny and newly bound – it actually felt to Tom as if he was the first person to ever touch it. He turned a few pages and was surprised to find that he was able to read some of the words. He had expected it to be written in Latin.

'It's in some form of English,' he whispered, passing the book to his sister. 'The spellings are quite strange though.'

'And it's not very big, is it?' she replied.

'It must be written in some form of Old English,' he said. 'But at least ordinary people can understand it.'

'People like us you mean?'

'People exactly like us.'

Tom took the Bible back and managed to squeeze it into his

jacket pocket. 'Let's keep it,' he said, 'just in case.'

'You're like a walking bookshelf,' tutted Emma in mock disapproval, but her attention had turned again to the Cathedral itself. She was gazing around at the walls, windows and ceiling. The building seemed to have lost some of its magic and sparkle for it no longer shone with the decoration and colour as it had done previously. Gone were most of the wonderful paintings and patterns and missing too were many of the colourful stained glass windows – they had mostly been replaced with plain ones. And it dawned on her that there seemed to be no trace of the monks – they had seemingly vanished into thin air too. 'What has happened?' she asked, in a state of shock. 'Why have things changed so much?' Jack began to sing once more with much seriousness in his voice:

Some people said the Cathedral must be plain
while others refused and wanted colour again;
so the times were hostile and much anger was spread
and many would suffer, their blood being shed.

'What times were hostile?' asked Tom straight away. 'What year are we in now? And who's blood was shed??' He didn't much like the sound of any of this. Jack seemed to be saying that many people disagreed over whether or not there should be decoration inside the Cathedral. Perhaps the same people also disagreed over whether the monks should live there. Maybe even some of them didn't want the Bible to be written in English. Yet what frightened

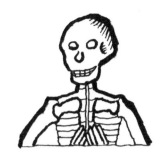

Tom was that these same people seemed to be prepared to argue and even fight one another for how they thought the Cathedral should look. They probably fought over all the other churches as well. 'Why couldn't they just decide what to do by talking rather than fighting?' Tom blurted out. 'I mean it's not a big deal is it, deciding whether you want a place decorated or not? I don't want to be caught up in any violent arguments!' But Jack wasn't listening; he had already wandered away. 'I bet the serpents are still here though,' Tom added as an afterthought.

As he moved along the aisle away from the pulpit, he saw Jack standing ahead of him, motionless and with a peculiar, almost wicked glint in his eye. His face was twisted and distorted. Tom felt his stomach churn and a sense of foreboding once more came over him.

'Thisssss,' hissed the Clock-Jack out of nothingness, 'thisss fate awaits you both!' He slowly pointed to the stone wall and then darted away in an instant. Tom looked to see what was there and recoiled when he saw the smiling face of a skeleton peering back at him. He steadied himself and under his breath whispered a reassurance. 'Remember what Brother Nicholas said – the serpents can possess the unwary to divide us from each other; it's not Jack's fault.' He looked again at the skeleton. 'It's not his fault...' the words trailed away as he saw that a verse had been inscribed beneath the skeleton's ribs. 'Emma, Emma, this could be it – the verse I mean.' His voice wobbled. He hadn't noticed that she was now standing right behind him, unable to move or to speak as she stared at the carving and the verse below. Tom began to read, his voice unsteady and hushed:

All you that do this place pass bye
Remember death for you must dye
As you are now even so was I
And as I am so shall you be

'And as I am so shall you be,' repeated Tom.

'I don't like it,' whispered Emma, 'I don't want to be like that anytime soon.'

'It's not the verse we need.'

'How do you know?'

Tom had remembered something he had seen quite a while ago now — a sketch of this particular skeleton somewhere in the green leather book. He took time to find it and then showed Emma. 'Look!' he pointed and then added, 'and see what's written underneath.'

Thomas Gooding's memorial
by Obidiah Barebones
time traveller & musician
PS this is not the verse for the time traveller!

'This can't be the verse for us either, or any time traveller come to that. It's probably just a memorial; maybe the serpents are trying to frighten us again.'

'It's how they intend us to end up more like – as skeletons stuck here forever. Come on Tom, let's go, I don't like it.'

As Emma disappeared, Tom decided to linger for a moment. The more he studied the memorial, the more he found that he actually quite liked it. It was having the opposite effect to the one the serpents had intended. Tom felt the smiling skeleton to be strangely reassuring. One day in the distant future this fate awaited them all, he knew that of course – no one can live forever. Yet he was growing ever more determined that the serpents would not bring that day any closer.

'Dust to dust,' he muttered to himself, turning away from the memorial. As he did so, a cold, ghostly air once again enveloped him. Through it came a clear, deathly whisper; 'Watch your time – and add it to nine.' The coldness engulfed him for a moment and then it was gone. He searched frantically for Emma.

'Did you hear it?' he trembled, his voice showing a mixture of excitement and fear. She was sheltering beside the pulpit and had turned very pale. She was deep in concentration and for some reason, was studying her watch. 'Did you hear it?' Tom repeated.

'Seven minutes past seven,' she whispered, her mind whirring. 'That's fourteen in total. Then, add it to nine and you get twenty three. Tom – it's twenty three.'

'What is?' he said, utterly baffled.

'The answer to Brother Nicholas' riddle,' she said excitedly.

'What?'

'The time on my watch is seven past seven — it's been stuck at the time ever since we were in the river gatehouse with Dad. It's been stuck like that for a reason! Two sevens are fourteen, add them to nine as Brother Nicholas keeps saying and it makes twenty three. Look, I don't know what it means either, just write it down in the book will you?'

He hurriedly found the page on to which he had previously written a wobbly number nine and scribbled 23 next to it:

9:23

It seemed to make sense to put the two numbers together. He now had 9:23 — what could that possibly mean? Was it the time at which they should arrive at the north door to face the three serpents?

Chapter Twelve

Thrown to the Fire

As they stood rooted to the spot in the centre of the now very plain and almost colourless Cathedral, there was an almighty crash on the great west doors. Tom spun round, terrified. Emma yelled out 'Jack — what on earth was that?' A hurried rhyme was given in reply:

Time is rushing onwards
and we must move fast,
for the Civil War is coming
— another hundred years have passed!

'How could a war ever be civil?' she replied as another almighty blow struck the west doors. It was followed by a whole series of violent bangs, thumps and crashes. The chains locking the two doors together were jolted into life as each heavy blow caused them to jump and dance. They were forced up and then came crashing back down noisily on to the solid wood as the doors themselves shook in their frame. The attack was gathering in violence. 'We must keep safe,' Tom shouted to his sister as he motioned for them to hide behind one of the giant pillars in the Nave.

From there Tom just about caught sight of the giant wooden doors burst open under the pressure and the chains shatter from the force of all the blows upon them. He looked on aghast as he saw a great mob surge into the building, shouting, spitting and venting their fury at – well, Tom didn't quite know what they were so angry about. There must have been hundreds of people in the crowd. Some looked like ordinary citizens; others perhaps were city officials wearing fancy golden chains and woollen black coats with grey breeches.

He even saw some soldiers near the back wearing tin pot helmets and breast plates. They were carrying huge wooden pikes which swayed dangerously in the air. Tom gasped as he spotted two musketeers who appeared to be smoking pipes and swigging from tankards of ale. He turned to Jack and Emma but saw that they too were terrified by the sight before them. Although there was much anger in the crowd, the people seemed to know exactly what they were doing. Very carefully and very deliberately they started to take down and remove the last remaining pictures, paintings and decorations from the Cathedral.

Tom saw a small group taking down all the crucifixes that they could find and stared in amazement as some of the soldiers started to tear down the organ. They thrust their towering pikes into its belly, ripping out all the pipes so that they came crashing down on to the floor. One of the soldiers picked up a fallen pipe and tooted on it mockingly. Then suddenly a small explosion echoed around the building. Tom jumped and then remembered the musketeers. 'They're firing muskets!' he shouted in alarm. A cloud of grey smoke rose from the area of the Choir.

His feet took off before he had time to think. Dashing from behind the pillar, Tom ran underneath the organ – managing to dodge the pikemen still busy with their task — and arrived just in time to see one of the musketeers take aim and fire his musket at one of the brightly painted tombs. The musket ball exploded into it, sending a shower of stone shrapnel and dust high into the air. The trooper laughed, took a swig of ale from his tankard and took aim again. Tom dived for the floor. It was a scene of utter chaos, but somehow it seemed to be orderly chaos, if such a thing was possible. 'What's happening?' he shouted to Jack, managing to rejoin them behind the pillar. Their little companion took a deep breath and shouted in his loudest voice:

> The Civil War raging throughout the land
> I have always found hard to fully understand.
> King Charles on the one side, Parliament on the other
> meant father fought son and brother killed brother.

There really was no time for a history lesson now — they were in real danger from a mob that seemed intent on destroying everything in the Cathedral. 'But why are these people here now?' he yelled across to Jack. But Jack couldn't answer. In a flash he was swept off his feet by one of the tough looking soldiers who had been ripping the organ apart. The soldier clutched Jack roughly around the waist and marched him off towards the west doors. 'Jack!' screamed Emma after the Clock-Jack and then; 'Leave him alone you pig,' as she charged off after the soldier.

Tom had no option but to follow as most of the mob now headed out of the west doors with them. In his confusion, he struggled to see his sister and the soldier who had captured Jack. He was in the middle of the huge crowd, amongst people carrying organ pipes, crucifixes, paintings and even some of the fine clothes that must have been worn by the priests. Where the crowd was going and what would happen to all these things, Tom had no idea. All he cared about was finding his sister and his companion Jack again. It was just as well that no-one seemed to notice him. He screamed at the top of his voice and jostled and pushed his way through the crowd, but all seemed in vain for he heard no reply nor caught sight of them.

Tom suddenly felt a terrible realisation. If he lost his sister now, there would be no way that he could face the three serpents alone.

Eventually the noisy and angry crowd came to a halt. The mass of people was seething with rage and hostility, but somehow Tom managed to fight and struggle his way to the front. He saw that the crowd had gathered around a giant bonfire, which had been set up in the centre of the City market place, near the chequered looking flint Guildhall. The bonfire was ready to be lit. He was stunned to see the people begin to throw everything they had taken from the Cathedral on to the great pile of wood stacked up in the centre. They were actually going to burn it all right there in front of him!

At that moment one of the citizens stepped forward – he was carrying a burning torch and as he lowered it to the base of the bonfire a great cheer went up from the crowd. It caught quickly and in no time at all the flames were dancing high and bright as everything brought from the Cathedral was devoured by the hungry fire. Tom clutched the antique leather book tightly under his jacket, for he was terrified that it too would be thrown on to the blazing inferno. With the heat and noise of the flames growing ever more intense, he gazed anxiously across to the crowd on the other side of the fire and was jolted instantly out of his thoughts. Three rows back stood Emma, Jack and the soldier, all staring intently at the growing fire before them.

His relief turned instantly to horror as the soldier once again bent down to pick up the little Clock-Jack, as if to throw him on to the fire. 'Noooo!' screamed Tom, racing towards them and narrowly avoiding the hissing flames which seemed to greedily reach out to try and grab him. 'Leave him alone – we need him!' Tom yelled, crashing into the sturdy soldier and almost knocking him to the ground.

Recoiling in dazed confusion, Tom looked up to see the soldier not, as expected, throwing the Clock-Jack on to the hungry fire, but rather hoisting him up on to his shoulders in order to get a better view. 'But...but, I don't understand,' stammered Tom. 'You want to throw him on the fire...don't you?' At this, the soldier let out an enormous laugh that shook his shoulders so violently that Jack bobbed up and down on top of them. 'Throw Master Jack on to the fire?' chuckled the soldier. 'Burn one of my best friends? I've been accused of many things, but that's the worst of the lot!'

Tom could also hear a high pitched giggling coming from Jack himself and feeling rather silly, turned to Emma for support. She widened her eyes as if to say 'cool it Tom.' She cleared her throat and explained. 'Apparently, this is Captain Livewell Loveday, soldier of Parliament and defender of the people's just rights and liberties.'

Tom raised his eyebrows. Apart from the soldier's name, he hadn't understood a word of what Emma had just said. And the name was unusual enough. 'Defender of the people's cold nights and fisheries...' he muttered to himself.

'Oh dear,' said Emma, obviously frustrated with her brother. 'Captain Loveday is fighting on the side of Parliament against King Charles I. It's this Civil War. Jack and he go back a long way apparently — something about fighting together in Scotland, I think.'

Tom looked at the soldier and then at Jack perched high up on his shoulders. He noticed that they were both wearing matching red tunics with shiny brass buttons down the front. He knew how much Emma disliked the idea of warfare and so he plucked up the courage to ask Captain Loveday a question himself. 'If you're a soldier,' he quizzed, 'why were you attacking the Cathedral when there was no-one there to defend it?'

Suddenly they were oblivious to the crowd and bonfire burning just a few metres in front of them. Captain Loveday became very serious and Tom wished that he hadn't challenged him. The soldier frowned and stroked his rough bristly chin as he thought before answering 'In this year of our Lord 1643, I am fighting for our Parliament against King Charles and all his evil advisers...' he paused. 'A King who takes taxes from us that we should not pay. A King who forces us to worship in ways that we do not want...'

The soldier waited for a moment and then continued. 'We do not want images and decorations in our churches which only distract us from worship. Our worship should be based on the words of the Bible, not on silly pictures, carvings and superstitions.'

Looking straight at Tom and pointing his finger he said hoarsely: 'Remember to read your Bible boy! Remember to read your Bible!' He then turned angrily back towards the fire, throwing on a large wooden crucifix for good measure.

Tom had always quite liked the pictures, paintings and carvings in the Cathedral, especially the roof bosses and the stories they told. He thought it was a great shame that many of them were now being burnt and destroyed forever. But on the other hand if Captain Loveday and many of the people of Norwich did not want their churches to be full of decoration then perhaps they were right to clear them away. Whatever the case, he thought it was sad that people could not allow each other to worship in whatever way they chose.

As the smoke from the fire became ever thicker around them, Tom struck upon a good idea. Why not build some new churches in the city for all the people who did not like decorations and pictures to get in the way? These new churches could have clear white walls and be simple and plain which would allow the people to focus on their study of the Bible without getting distracted. The older churches and the Cathedral could then be left alone for all those who still liked to have images and decorations as part of their worship.

As he thought this over, he turned to watch the violent dancing of the fire and rather absentmindedly reached in to his pocket for the small leather book. As far as he could tell, it contained no references whatsoever to this particular episode with Captain Livewell Loveday and the roaring bonfire with its fuel of Cathedral paintings and crucifixes. Perhaps the previous time travellers had not experienced this bit. Or maybe they had been too afraid to risk the book being seen. Tom turned the page and froze with horror. Staring back at him from the page, shakily yet unmistakably written, were the words:

Under No circumstances Must you let Captain Livewell Loveday see this book!

Tom moved, but it was too late. Towering above him, his face suddenly red with rage stood Captain Loveday. The soldier yelled with such might that he almost drowned out the roaring of the fire.

'The superstitious book!' he bellowed. 'This foolish boy has the superstitious book! Take it from him — it must be sacrificed to the fire!!' Those stood immediately around turned in an instant to see what all the commotion was about. As Captain Loveday yelled again, many others began to move towards them. 'What's that you say Livewell?' shouted a stubbly, rough looking man dressed all in black.

Jack, who had all this time remained perched on top of Captain Loveday's shoulders, observed the scene with dismay. He looked on aghast as the crowd gathered round and started to become boisterous, pushing and shoving the two children. 'The superstitious book,' repeated the soldier and made a lunge towards Tom, trying to grab it as he went. 'The boy has the book. It must be destroyed!'

Tom managed to sidestep away and backed in to the crowd, desperately trying to stuff the book back in to his jacket. But there were too many people and he became entangled in a sea of clutching, snatching hands. 'Emma!' he yelled at the top of his voice, as the ranting soldier bore down on him. But she too was becoming ensnared. At that moment, Jack decided to act. Best friend or not, he grasped tightly on to Captain Loveday's wide brimmed felt hat and pulled it firmly down over his eyes. The soldier let out a scream of fury and shook Jack violently off his shoulders, causing him to clatter noisily to the ground. 'Betrayed, I am betrayed!' he roared. 'Throw them all to the fire! Be done with them. Do not let them escape!' Yet the children had seen their chance. As the furious soldier staggered and swayed, trying to pull his hat back up over his eyes, they darted away, nimbly avoiding the grasping hands that reached out for them. In his furious efforts to catch them, the soldier only succeeded in crashing blindly into his fellow citizens, causing them to scatter wildly. So Jack too made his escape, sprinting through the legs of the angry mob gathered around him. And they were aided further in their escape. For the black clouds of smoke from the bonfire had by now become so dense that the soldiers and the citizens could barely see one another, let alone the diminutive fugitives. As they raced back in the direction of the Cathedral, Tom could hear the hissing, spitting and crackling of the flames mingled with the roar of the crowd. There was fury as the mob realised that the children and the book had eluded them.

Chapter Thirteen

The Knights of the Window

Tom collapsed in an untidy heap and gasped for breath. Emma and Jack lay sprawled out beside him on the west steps of the Cathedral, panting, coughing and spluttering. He rolled over to look back through the giant gateway that led out into the City. He half expected the furious mob to burst through at any moment. And yet everything was quiet and still. After several minutes, when he was convinced that Captain Loveday and the angry citizens had not followed them from the marketplace, he dusted himself down and retrieved the ancient leather book.

As he glanced through it silently, Tom shook his head as he realised how this small object had almost cost them their lives. He thought about what Jack had just done – saved them from the mob and from a terrible fate. And Jack had lost Captain Loveday forever as a friend in the process. He looked affectionately over to the little Clock-Jack who was still recovering from his ordeal. Turning to the second page, he found Nathaniel Rowbottom's sketch of Jack. Underneath it was written: 'Jack – a trusted companion – of sorts!' Tom smiled as he blotted out the words 'of sorts' from the page. 'Jack – a trusted companion,' he whispered under his breath, happy with his work.

His thoughts again focussed on what they had just experienced. In particular he thought about what Captain Loveday had said to him moments before the soldier had tried to destroy the book and throw them all on the bonfire. 'Remember to read your Bible boy!' The soldier's words were loud and vivid in his mind. He mulled it over. Was the soldier giving something away? Tom found the page where he had scribbled 9:23 and wrote above it, 'Remember to read your Bible.' The page now looked like this;

Remember to read your Bible
9:23

This still made little sense, but it seemed right. And he sensed that their confrontation with the serpents was drawing very close.

'I half expected the Cathedral to be gone,' groaned Emma as she got to her feet, recovered from her recent sprint. 'I thought that bunch might have destroyed the lot.' Her face lit up. 'And the serpents with it!'

'And the North Door and our means of escape,' Tom said hastily.

'I hadn't thought of that.'

'It actually looks in really good condition to me,' he said, standing and nearly bumping into a party of very well dressed ladies who were chatting away excitedly as they hurried past.

'It has been repaired and restored,' mused Emma, staring intently at the stonework around the great west doors. Yet Tom wasn't listening — his attention had followed the group of smartly dressed ladies.

'Cakes on legs,' he giggled, looking at their beautiful dresses, which were very frilly and especially puffy around the waist. Before they entered the building, the ladies lowered the small white umbrellas they were holding, but decided to keep their dainty little floral hats on. Whoever they were, Tom thought they must be quite rich; they certainly didn't look as if they were part of a mob on its way to attack and demolish things.

They took the decision to follow the small party of ladies inside. It was immediately apparent that nearly all of the decoration had indeed gone – Captain Loveday and his followers had been successful in that task. What struck them most of all about this was that they were now able to see the creamy coloured stone of the walls once again. This was the fine stone that they had seen being unloaded from the great boats that had sailed right in through Pull's Ferry. 'Tom,' his sister nudged him in the ribs and pointed, 'Those are the doors smashed down by the angry mob!'

As Tom studied the doors in amazement – they were now repaired and back in place – he noticed some activity above. He peered up to see a team of glaziers working ever so carefully to construct a huge new stained glass window. A giant scaffold had been erected in front of the window. Tom winced as he saw the image of a green serpent coiling around a cross; it was being put together in the central lower section of the window. He took a deep breath and steadied himself; 'this is the west door,

not the north.' There were other pictures too, all forming part of a whole. The window looked as if it was going to show a range of different stories when complete.

Moving quickly away, they saw small groups of visitors wandering around pointing, chatting and admiring the architecture of the building. Some were talking in hushed tones while others were simply marvelling at what they saw.

As Tom, Emma and Jack made their way slowly around the Cathedral it became clear that these were tourists, come to admire such a magnificent place. As well as these visitors there were all sorts of workmen around the building, constructing and repairing the stonework, glass and wood. At last the Cathedral seemed to be receiving the right kind of attention. They stopped in an area where there was a great deal of activity. Jack beckoned to one of the workmen with an excited wave of his arm. As the man approached, Tom realised that he was in fact not one of the workers at all. By the look of his elegant long coat, tall black hat, fine waistcoat and golden pocket watch, he was probably in charge of all that was going on around them. By way of introduction, Jack began to sing:

The year 1835 saw the Victorians here
to repair and restore and bring us good cheer;
the man now in charge, Mr Salvin, I know.
Tell us your plans for soon we must go!

On hearing this, the well dressed gentleman removed his hat and bowed to them in a sweepingly elegant manner. 'Good day to you, Jack,' said Mr Salvin. 'What a pleasure to have you with us once again. Perhaps you will be so kind as to introduce me to your companions.' Jack looked delighted at this suggestion and replied:

Tom and Emma my friends close and true
who have seen such things as never they knew;
soon they will face their greatest test
so help Mr Salvin, help with their quest!

Mr Salvin smiled kindly and leaned forward to shake Tom and Emma by the hand. 'Yes, yes,' he said, 'I will show you what we have been doing here; it may indeed help you with your quest!' And with that he motioned for them to follow.

'You must understand that this building is over seven hundred and fifty years old and has experienced much in its lifetime. You name it and at some time or another it has probably happened right here in Norwich Cathedral! So much so in fact that the building is now in urgent need of repair. Fires, storms, riots and rebellions, you know the sort of thing.'

'He's not wrong there,' Emma nudged Tom 'and we've experienced most of them!'

'We are repairing the crumbling stonework both inside and outside and my highly skilled team of glaziers is constructing the magnificent west window,' Mr Salvin explained. He motioned flamboyantly towards the west doors. They came to a halt in one of the side Chapels. 'This is the Jesus Chapel,' he said proudly, 'and if you look carefully you will see how my men have restored the artwork put there originally by Herbert de Losinga and his monks.'

Sure enough, there up above them, freshly repainted onto the stonework, were great swirls of bright colours – beautiful patterns in red, green and gold.

Mention of the monks refocused Tom's mind on Brother Nicholas once again and he wondered if the friendly monk would like to see his Cathedral restored with its original decoration. 'How do you know what the original artwork was like?' Tom asked. 'Perhaps they have some help from a little friend,' Emma interjected, nodding towards Jack who was chatting animatedly with Mr Salvin by the Chapel entrance.

'We have plans and maps you see,' said Mr Salvin, 'that show us what the building was like before. Some of them are hundreds of years old and very brittle – we have to be extremely careful'. He mulled this over for a moment and then reached for his golden pocket watch, studying it intently. 'Infuriating – it's stopped again. It keeps doing that you know, usually just after seven o'clock...it's a mystery it really is. Now where was I? Oh yes, the maps...' He tapped his watch and frowned. 'You see there has always been one map that has eluded us. It's been missing for centuries. Torn out of its book and discarded...'

Tom could hear his heart hammering inside his rib cage.

'Yes, it is rumoured to show the original Cathedral building, constructed from 1096, with all its secret passage ways, labyrinths and tunnels. A fine map of much worth apparently. But it's not just the Cathedral it shows. Oh no indeed. There are all sorts of other ancient buildings and sites marked on it as well — sites and buildings from this great City of ours. A real treasure map apparently. It was owned by two brothers. Some mumbo jumbo about them fighting serpents for the map, but only one of them managing to escape. The serpents imprisoned the other one and the brothers have been separated ever since. I don't believe that part of the story myself actually, but the map I think.....well it would be wonderful to see it. Be very valuable I imagine.'

'Where did they imprison him?' asked Tom, scarcely able to believe what he was hearing.

'Only the map can answer that,' replied Mr Salvin, in a thoughtful voice. 'The serpents were desperate to keep the brothers apart you see...now why was that?' He broke off and scratched his head.

'The City of Light Mr Salvin sir,' shouted one of the workmen from inside the Chapel.

'Ah yes, yes that's it. Well done James! Yes, legend has it that the serpents were desperate to keep them apart because if they were ever reunited, the brothers would chime together once again and usher in a new City of Light. I'm not sure how they'd do that mind you, chiming together sounds rather odd doesn't it? The only way I can see them doing it is by being part of a clock, I suppose like our little friend Jack here...' he said, his eyes narrowing on the Clock-Jack stood next to him. 'Mmmm...yes, well anyway, this would banish all evil from the world and establish goodness and love in the new City. That's the light part of it you understand – light and love banishing darkness and evil. Now that really would be quite something eh?'

The children said nothing.

'Still' Mr Salvin continued with a sharp intake of breath, 'it would be quite a task, creating this City I mean. The serpents were rumoured to be only the tip of the iceberg as far as the forces of evil went. There were plenty of creatures more fearsome than serpents who would certainly oppose any City of Light. The brothers and their allies would have to battle with them! There's a lot more to the story, but it escapes me know. Forgive me.' And with that he sat down, mopping his forehead with a bright red polka dot handkerchief.

'Chiming together to create the City,' whispered Emma.

'Something more fearsome than the serpents...' replied Tom.

A loud crash suddenly came from a short distance away, causing all four of them to jump with fright. Surely there was not going to be any more rioting or trouble when everything at last seemed so calm and peaceful inside the building? They walked briskly over towards the commotion only to see a large cloud of dust rising in the air and hear hoots of laughter coming from the gathering workmen.

'That's the last time you'll try and take tea to the top of the scaffolding, Mark,' laughed one of the glaziers to his colleague below. In his efforts to take six cups of tea and a plate of sandwiches upwards, Mark had only succeeded in collapsing nearly half of the wooden scaffolding around him. Fortunately no-one seemed injured. Mark had turned an embarrassed shade of red but couldn't help joining in with the laughter of his workmates. As Tom surveyed the scene with a large grin on his face, he caught Mark's eye – the workman was staring directly at him. Mark – he had seen that written somewhere in the leather book; it was the only name from the list of four that had not been crossed through.

There was something beyond as well. Peering through the half demolished scaffolding, Tom could just about make out three rather mysterious figures in a large stained glass window. This was the window the glaziers had been working on. As the dust cleared a little, he saw that the figures seemed to be knights, dressed in various shades of green, brown and red. They were youthful and full of life. And utterly mesmerising. Each carried a spear, although one of the knights appeared to be holding something bigger – a lance perhaps. And they all wore armour on various parts of their bodies. Two of them were protected by patterned breastplates and carried sturdy looking leather shields, one of which was a beautiful deep red colour. Tom studied each figure carefully. They were stunningly beautiful. He had not seen them, or a sketch, or a description of them anywhere in the book. But he did remember the creaky old sign at Pull's Ferry. 'The Knights of the Window' he breathed, enchanted.

The knights seemed to have been created from the ground itself; to have grown from the very earth they stood upon. They were entwined with the natural world; had come from the very elements themselves. Somehow he knew these three green knights fought for what was right and good and that they would always stand up against evil.

As he came out of his reverie, Tom helped himself to some of the fresh tea and sandwiches that the workmen had provided. He couldn't help but notice that Mark was still staring intently at him. This made Tom feel decidedly uncomfortable. He couldn't think of anything to say but the workman kept on staring. Then a smile broke out on Mark's face and he nodded at Tom and then at Emma. He paused and then turned quietly back to his work.

Tom grabbed the leather book and scribbled the name Mark next to the numbers 9:23;

Remember to read your Bible
9:23 Mark

He caught one last glimpse of Mark, now standing in front of the three heroic knights of the window, before the workman hurried away to find a means of clearing up the mess he had created. Jack was tugging aggressively at his sleeve. 'What is it Jack?' snapped Tom with irritation, as the Clock-Jack pulled him away from the window and away from the three knights. They moved from the light of the window in to the darkened belly of the building.

Chapter Fourteen

The Three Serpents

For some time now a thought had been disturbing Emma. And yet she still had not mentioned anything to Tom. If they really were, as it seemed, travelling through time, then it was logical to think that at some point they would ultimately catch up with themselves in the present day. It was entirely possible that at some stage in this process they would bump into their father, not as they knew him now (although she was desperate for that to happen), but as a much younger man. And if that happened, there was the strong possibility that he would be with someone, a person not enshrined in the countless photos scattered across their small terraced house, or a person kept safe in the precious silver locket hanging around Emma's neck. No, this someone would at last be living and breathing and loving. It would be the mother about whom Emma only had the very faintest of memories.

છ

All was black and still around them. The heavy silence was only punctuated by Jack's rhythmic ticking. It made Tom feel that the time must be drawing near. 'You must give the serpents your verse at precisely the right moment and only then can you return' — he heard the voice of Brother Nicholas ringing in his ears.

The three of them stood lonely, shrouded in the solitude of the night. Tom felt incredibly tired — so much had happened to them and his body now needed to stop. Yet he doubted whether they would be able to rest. As he leaned for support on a plain wooden table, he heard Jack stumble forward in the blackness. Standing up on tiptoe, the Clock-Jack managed to locate the large iron handle of an ancient wooden door and with a grunting effort, succeeded in turning it. As the door creaked open, it let in a blast of icy cold air.

'Why do that?' Tom questioned. 'It's much warmer in here.' But the Clock-Jack ignored him and rapidly disappeared into the night, leaving the children standing there unsure as to what to do. As they peered into the blackness to try and locate him, the whole sky suddenly burst into light as if a million torches had all been switched on at once. They recoiled instantly, shielding their eyes. The intense white light was such a contrast to the darkness of only a few minutes before that they were momentarily blinded. As their eyes gradually became accustomed to it, they saw huge beams of light shooting upwards and searching across the sky. The beams swept backwards and forwards as if trying to detect something that might be hiding up there. What they were looking for was difficult to tell, but at least the beams had given enough light to illuminate Jack, who was standing only a few metres in front of them, fidgeting nervously. He beckoned them anxiously over and shouted:

Hurry for now is the Second World War
a war of destruction like never before;
we must now get you home before it's too late
follow me here and decide your...

For the first time since they had known him, Jack was unable to finish his rhyme. Instead his words were obliterated as a thunderous drone of airborne machines appeared from nowhere, drowning out his little voice and covering the night sky like a swarm of flies. Tom looked up and saw the searchlights, for that is what they surely were, focus on a mass of black aeroplanes as they came crawling towards them.

'Bombers,' he said slowly, 'come to destroy Norwich. Come on, we need shelter and we need it now!'

The sound of the massed planes was terrifying, almost deafening, and it became impossible to even hear one another shout.

Acting on pure instinct alone, Tom grabbed Emma by the hand and hoisted Jack up to carry him. He ran as fast as he could as the first bombs started to fall. He was not sure where he was going but something drew him on, as if a distant, familiar voice was calling to him, almost guiding him to the place. Distant echoes of conversations echoed through his head. As he ran he looked upwards and saw tiny black sticks falling from the open bellies of the aeroplanes. The first bomb made a whizzing sound as it came hurtling down and exploded not far away, shattering a group of giant yew trees and throwing a huge pile of earth up in to the air. Another came screaming towards them and landed closer this time, setting a house on fire only metres away from the Cathedral itself. Some of the planes were closer now and Tom caught a glimpse of one for a moment, frozen in the glare of a searchlight. Painted on its side and clearly visible, were three twisted, terrible black serpents.

Emma yelled in terror, a sound which only served to strengthen Tom's determination. As he rounded a corner he could see beyond the Cathedral and towards the city. It was a devastating sight. The whole of Norwich seemed to be ablaze. Bombs were falling like rain, sirens were wailing and the red, orange and gold of the many fires lit up the night sky completely. It was not something that Tom wanted to look at for long because it was a scene of death, destruction and misery. The bombs seemed to be hissing down on to the City and he couldn't help but think that the serpents would be laughing with delight at this scene. A City of Light would never be created in the midst of a ferocious war bringing evil, pain and suffering.

He turned frantically back towards the Cathedral – several voices now seemed to be calling him there. These voices were no longer reassuring or friendly, but they were pulling him to the same place. 'Tom, come to usssss, come to usssss!' Still clutching Emma and Jack firmly to him, Tom stumbled in through the west doors and headed along the north aisle. Outside, fires were raging throughout the City as the bombing raid grew in intensity. It was a miracle that the Cathedral itself had not been hit. Turning left at the end of the north aisle, he came into an area of the building that he did not recognise.

And then he stopped dead in his tracks. Ahead, shining and sinister through the misty, yellow gloom were three pairs of piercing green eyes.

Emma and Jack disentangled themselves and drew up on either side of Tom. Jack stood to his left, Emma on his right.

'We three sssee you,' came a clear, unnerving hiss.

Emma began to sob.

'You have entered the lair of the three serpents. What business do you have here?' the voice demanded as it rose in fury. But fear had paralysed them; they were unable to answer and stayed rooted to the spot. As the gloom cleared a little, the awful truth became clear. Perched high above them on the stone wall and leering down were three terrible, beastly serpent heads. The central head was situated above a locked door, which was set in a grand stone arch. Tom recognised it immediately as the strong and impressive looking door engraved on the cover of the book. 'The... the north door,' stuttered Emma, almost unable to say the words now that they were finally here. She glanced at Tom; 'Is it time for us to return?'

He knew in his heart that the moment had come, but that they were not prepared to face the serpents. What verse could he give to them when they hissed their demands? He had no idea. The central head spoke again. 'Travellers! We are the guardians of the north door and we have been waiting for you. None shall pass below!! If you have no verse to give us then the north door will remain locked forever. You will never travel homewards!'

Tom suddenly felt his courage swell up and he took a deep breath. 'We have the verse!' he shouted back defiantly, as Emma and Jack both stared at him in disbelief.

'Then let us have it!' spat the serpents together in what sounded like an evil chuckle, as if they sensed he was bluffing. But Tom didn't have the verse and he knew it. He had to play for time.

'How can we be sure that you will keep your word and let us through?' he shouted back at the scaly heads.

'Foolish boy!' screamed the central serpent. 'You dare to question us? You have failed in your mission and you still question?' and with that it began to quiver and twist violently. The other two heads also began to shake menacingly. The serpent facing Emma cried out. 'We shall always keep the brothers apart! And if you have no verse to give us then you must remain here forever!'

Tom instinctively reached for the leather book. He searched through it in a frenzy, tearing a few of the pages in the process. He found his scribbled notes, the ones he had felt should go together;

Remember to read your Bible
9:23 Mark

'What does this mean, what does this mean?' He sobbed and looked up to see the central serpent open its mouth and with it expose two rows of razor sharp teeth. Tom recoiled in horror as he recognised a rotting human head lodged firmly in the serpent's jaws. It was a truly terrible sight — the victim was young and must have been a previous time traveller who had failed in his task.

'No,' Tom yelled at the serpent in anger. 'That will not happen to us!' The eyes of the central serpent head flashed green as it began to detach itself from the wall. Tom screamed over to his sister, 'I need a Bible, Emma — find me a Bible!'

'Tom — you already have one,' she yelled back instantly: 'Remember — you picked it up and stuffed it in your pocket — a walking bookcase! Hurry,' she cried as the other two serpent heads detached themselves from the wall and hissed with glee.

Tom dug deeper into his jacket pocket and pulled out the small leather- bound Bible. His mind was racing. He must read the Bible as Captain Loveday had told him, but which part? He agonised. He knew that the Bible was divided up into sections called books and that each had been given a name. Looking desperately at his notes he saw the name Mark.

'Mark — the book of Mark,' he shouted at no-one in particular. That must be it! He had the name written down right there in front of him and next to it the numbers. 'Chapters and verses...chapters and verses,' he said without thinking. 'Yes! The book of Mark, chapter nine, verse 23! Please...'

Emma shrieked. The three serpent heads were now fully detached and were moving towards them, trailing long black scaly bodies as they advanced. Their jaws opened to show dripping, merciless fangs, glistening coldly in the half light. 'You will remain here with usssss forever!' hissed the central head just as Tom found his way to the book of Mark, chapter nine, verse 23. It was in a form of Old English; it was difficult to read, but not impossible. He screamed out the verse from the open page;

'All things are possible to those who believe!'

He screamed again, his lungs bursting as the serpents swooped down towards them.

'All things are possible to those who believe!'

The central head hissed with fury when it heard Tom's words.
'Their versssssse, the boy has their versssssse!' it screeched in agony, stopping only a few centimetres short of him. Its jaws dripped with saliva and its rancid, foul breath steamed over Tom.
'Urgghh!' Tom moaned as he backed away in disgust. He had seen again the remnants of the human head lodged deep in the serpent's jaws and had stared into its panicked, stricken eyes.
And then they heard it. It was a faint and confusing sound at first, but then it grew ever louder and clearer as it marched towards them. It was rhythmic and well paced and it was coming closer. It was the sound of footsteps, armoured footsteps. The clinking and the clanking of armoured feet and bodies on the cold stone floor was unmistakable. It rang and danced and echoed around the

building. It was the footsteps of knights. The central serpent swerved violently back towards the wall in a moment of panic. The other heads followed, spitting and screeching with rage.

'All things are possible to those who believe,' repeated Tom as loudly and clearly as he could.

The clanking footsteps quickened when Tom said this. He turned to see three magnificent knights dressed in beautiful shades of green, brown and red appear through the gloom. They were armoured, with helmets and patterned breastplates and carried spears, lances and shields. 'The three knights,' Tom gasped, 'of the window – I saw them before, Emma, before...' The shining knights marched on and drew up in front of Jack and the children, shielding and protecting them. They then turned so that they each faced one of the serpents.

By now the serpents had withdrawn fully to the wall and were no longer hissing and spiting, but seemed to be waiting, biding their time, ready to make their move.

Then without warning, the serpents joined together in one long, ear splitting cry. The two children clasped their hands over their ears to try and block the deafening sound, but it was no use, the sound seeped through and crippled them with agony. The noise was relentless and shattering. As he fell to the floor in a dizzying pain, Tom caught a glimpse of all three serpents detaching themselves from the wall at once and come hurtling towards the knights in a torrent of fury. The slithering serpents filled Tom with terror, but the three green warriors braced themselves, bravely standing their ground.

The knight standing in front of Emma raised his spear, drawing it back behind his head and then unleashed it in a blur. His powerful, muscular arm sent it zooming towards the approaching serpent. The spear flew through the air, slicing clean through the serpent's open jaws, shattering them and causing its lifeless head and neck to come crashing down on to the cold stone floor. It hit the floor with a thud, its slime and blood oozing everywhere.

To Tom's left, the knight before Jack had raised his shield in defence. He was just in time as the razor sharp teeth of the second serpent sank into its dark red leather. The sheer force of the impact caused the knight to stagger backwards, yet he managed to hold his footing. The terrible beast shook its head furiously, trying to detach itself and at the same time trying to knock the knight to the floor. Yet the green warrior was too alert and agile. With one powerful movement he pushed his shield to the floor, pinning the fearsome serpent underneath. With the serpent still attached, the knight thrust his lance through its writhing neck.

The loss of its two allies seemed to rouse the central serpent to even greater levels of anger. The sheer fury and power of its advance knocked the central knight clean off his feet and he came crashing back into Tom, sending him sprawling across the stone floor. The serpent saw its advantage and plunged its teeth deep into the knight's left arm. With its razor teeth, Tom was surprised that the serpent hadn't severed the arm completely. The knight cried in agony, dropping his shield to the floor. As the serpent rose and then descended to finish off its prey, the warrior managed to roll over and with his other arm, to raise his spear in defiance. The serpent was too late to alter its course. The knight held firm, piercing the evil neck just behind the head. As the serpent howled in agony it recoiled; its neck and head retracting rapidly towards the wall.

Even the other two serpents that had been slain were now drawn backwards, their heavy, lifeless bodies making a terrible writhing sound as they were pulled back across the floor. The sound was peculiar — something like a mass of chains being dragged across the cold stone floor. As the dead and dying serpents were drawn back, the knights too retreated, their shields, spears and armour again clinking and clanking as they went. They had been called for and they had performed their task heroically.

The two children stood there in awed silence, unable to summon any words whatsoever. The echoing footsteps of the knights grew ever fainter and then they were gone.

It was Jack who broke the silence:

The three earthly knights who awoke with the verse
were frozen before by the serpent's dread curse.
So the final victory that is yours now to own
means forever the serpents remain silent in stone!

They stared up at the serpent heads on the wall ahead of them. Whereas a moment ago the heads were alive with fury — hissing, spitting and screeching, their jaws open and ready to devour the children - they were now firmly locked into the wall and had indeed turned to stone. There they were – set above the north door, just as the picture on the front of the antique book had shown. And yet still, horribly clasped in the central serpent's jaws was the severed head of a previous time traveller. It too had now turned to stone.

There was an uneasy stillness. Emma drew a deep breath; she was sobbing with relief. She looked below the central, now stony head of the serpent. 'The north door,' she whispered, 'look Tom – the door is opening.' Beneath the serpent, the north door had indeed opened just a fraction and a chink of dazzling white light was shining through. Tom took a step backwards, fearful that this white light would be as intense and as blinding as that which they'd first experienced at the river gatehouse. But he needn't have worried. This light was calm and soothing and he felt instantly cradled and supported by it.

He reached out instinctively for Emma's hand and then for Jack, but the little Clock-Jack shunned it and turned away. He muttered:

> *The door is for you and through you must go,*
> *to return to your father as only you know.*
> *I still have my mission and find him I must*
> *For I am a companion in whom all can trust!*

'But Jack...' started Emma...

> *Hurry – time is short so I fear,*
> *leave while you can, but I must stay here.*

Emma rushed over and flung her arms around him, 'I'll always remember you Jack,' she said.

The north door was by now fully open and its glorious white light was streaming through.

'Jack — thanks for everything,' Tom blurted as he pulled his sister away. 'We'll see you again!'

As they ran towards the door, Tom wondered why he had said that — they weren't going to see Jack again; it was a silly thing to say.

ℰℐ

The door was wide open and the light coming from beyond it was magnificent. The children at last felt no fear. Instead they felt exactly the opposite. As they entered the glow streaming from the doorway they felt hope and for the first time in a long while they felt completely safe. They were home. It was as though someone was reaching out to them, to draw them close and protect them. As Tom walked through the doorway he turned to see Jack one last time, but the little Clock-Jack had gone and the Cathedral was still and quiet. He looked up to see a magnificent stained glass window towering above them, the smiling faces of mother and child there in reassurance. As he did so, the light caught the silver locket around Emma's neck in a brilliant, blinding flash. The light danced on the locket for a second and then was gone. It was in that moment that Tom knew she was there with them and that she had been all along, her arms open in love for her children.

The beautiful white light surrounded them completely in its brilliant glow as they moved through the doorway.

Chapter Fifteen

Return to the Gatehouse

Tom felt the warmth of a late summer breeze roll over him as he turned, sighed and slowly sat up. The sunlight was dancing on the gently swaying trees and the river looked serenely calm and still. His head was spinning. He began to replay every scene in detail.

Next to him lay his sister Emma, still fast asleep. Perhaps she too was dreaming. He looked around quickly for Jack and then remembered that they had left him on the other side of the north door.

His mind was alive with all that they had just experienced as everything flooded through him. The people they had met, especially Jack and Brother Nicholas, the situations they had found themselves in and the final battle between the heroic knights and the three serpents. He marvelled at how the clues they had found had led them to the Biblical verse. This had in turn awoken the three mighty warriors who had come to their aid and slain the serpents. It had certainly been a close run thing. Yet as he thought of those beasts, of their horrible heads and their evil fangs, he began to realise that they no longer terrified him. The courage of the knights had seen to that. He realised too that something had also changed deep within him. His mother had been the light beyond the north door and it was she who had created such intense feelings of safety and reassurance. They may never see her again, but she was there all the same. Tom had found a new feeling of belief; in his family, in friendship and in the power of good.

His thoughts were interrupted by the sound of familiar voices coming from the building that stood just beyond. As Emma awoke from her deep sleep, Tom saw their father striding energetically over towards them and another man walking more slowly behind him. It was the gatekeeper – of course, the gatekeeper Mr Postwick.

'Thomas! Emma!' bellowed Mr Buxton, 'what sleepyheads you are - you've been snoozing here for an absolute age! And I thought that I'd been off for quite some time! Goodness me' he added, shuffling his feet.

'Dad!!' yelled Emma, rushing up to him and flinging her arms around his neck.

'Steady on my darling,' he said, 'I'm pleased to see you too!'

As they disentangled themselves, Mr Buxton continued. 'You know I've had plenty of time for tea and cake with Mr Postwick here. He's told me all about this amazing place and the many stories it holds.' He gestured beyond them towards the silhouette of the Cathedral in the distance. 'I must tell you them sometime,' he added with a smile. Tom stuttered in confusion. 'Dad, we've been…we've been…' he struggled to explain. Where had they been

exactly and how could he possibly articulate it? Their father had been fast asleep himself when their journey had begun in the spinning sitting room and had missed the whole lot.

'Dad — have we got something to tell you,' Emma exclaimed — 'we've been battling with the three serpents!'

'You've been sleeping here like babies more like,' chuckled their father. 'That's what they've been doing all right; isn't that so Mr Postwick?' He turned to face the gatekeeper, who had held back from them a little. The old man was frail and his dusty red jacket with its brass buttons looked as if it had seen better days, but he had something very familiar about him. Perhaps it was the faded stripy short trousers or maybe it was the peculiar grey moustache that curled upwards at each end that was so familiar, but as Tom studied Mr Postwick carefully, he mouthed a silent 'Jack.' As he did so, he reached automatically for the leather book. But to his dismay it was nowhere to be found. He searched frantically in all his jacket and trouser pockets, turning them inside out in the process. Yet both the antique book and the Bible he had collected were gone.

He slumped to the ground. 'Emma, the book — the antique book...it's gone!' He gulped in dismay. 'The sketches, the clues —

all gone!'

'Oh dear, now come on, Tom, we can always get you another,' said his father as sympathetically as possible, sitting down next to him on the grass and not really sure what he was talking about. 'I mean, where did you get it from the first place?'

But Tom didn't answer. In his mind he was reliving the scene. The central knight had been knocked off his feet by the enraged serpent and they had both came crashing back in to him. He must have lost the book then. There was a moment of silence.

'Tom, you were never meant to keep it,' said Emma softly, putting a comforting arm around his shoulders. 'Remember what Brother Nicholas said; the book was owned by many before you – and will be found by many who follow. They will need it on their adventures and on their mission. You added your own experiences to what it already contained and that will help those who come after us.'

'It will?' interrupted Mr Buxton, a look of total confusion showing on his face.

'But I still don't really get why we had to go through all that in the first place,' pleaded Tom. 'Why would anyone – I mean what was the point of it all? All those clocks, the white light, Brother Nicholas, Jack, the serpents – why send us on that adventure, or mission or whatever any of them want to call it, if we have nothing to show for it?'

'Someone may one day find the missing map and succeed in the rescue mission I suppose,' she answered. 'And when the brothers are reunited' she paused, 'the City of Light will be created…It just wasn't us — we were never given the map and certainly didn't find it.

Mr Postwick remained rooted to the spot, some distance away. He viewed the scene with dismay, his moustache twitching nervously at either end. He looked at them for a moment longer his face sad and drawn and then he turned, shuffling slowly back towards the gatehouse. As he did so he croaked under his breath, fighting back the tears; 'You didn't find him then did you? You might have done alright for yourselves, but you didn't find him. You can't have done. I know you didn't find him because if you had then he would have come back with you.' He cleared his throat, and sobbed. 'The City is as far away as it ever was. We'll never create it…' He burst into a flood of tears as he disappeared.

The children turned in a flash to follow. But the old gatekeeper was gone and all that they heard was the gentle clinking of tea cups coming from the river gatehouse.

Chapter Sixteen

The Map of 12 Revealed

Tom sat in the living room of their small terraced house and stared at the television screen. He was only half listening to some news item about the possibility of getting cats to sing together in a choir, if only the prevailing winds were favourable. The reporter seemed to be getting very excited as she listened to a group of cats wailing away in a suburban garden somewhere. Tom flicked channels to an ice hockey game, but he couldn't settle his mind on anything. He kept thinking of the small leather book and wishing that he hadn't lost it. He knew that what Emma had told him was right — that the book was meant to be passed on from one traveller to the next to help them on their journey. And, he supposed, it would help them reunite the two brothers and create the City of Light that everyone kept going on about. He wondered for a moment if that City would be Norwich itself, or if it might be some far distant place that they knew nothing about. If only the map could be found...

Emma was also right when she said that they had actually gained a huge amount from their experiences. He knew, he felt, that he had become closer to his mother than ever before — he knew that she was there, watching and protecting. He had yearned for this for such a long time and it was wonderful. He was stronger for it and more confident and he felt a bond to his sister that had never existed before. Yet all this didn't stop him from wishing desperately that he had some memento from their adventure, some little scrap at least to hold and keep safe as a reminder.

And so he couldn't settle. There was actually something more immediate bugging him. He hadn't heard what Mr Postwick had said as he'd shuffled back to the gatehouse, but he was troubled by the fact that the gatekeeper had seemed bitterly disappointed and had in fact burst into tears upon seeing them both again.

'All right, Thomas,' said Mr Buxton as he came crashing into the room. 'What you up to?'

'Nothing much,' replied Tom despondently.

'I thought I might pop into town a little later — spot of shopping. An antique shop or two — a few things I could do with. You fancy it?'

Tom considered the invitation for a moment. 'I might give it a miss this time, Dad' he murmured, 'I'm still recovering from our last one.' And then added, 'but thanks anyway.'

He listened as his father noisily put on his shoes, rummaged in his coat pockets for something or other and tried to unlock the front door all at the same time.

'Oh, by the way,' he said, putting his head back round the door. 'I forgot to give you this — I got it from Mr Postwick. He said he meant to give it to you when we first met. He was awfully agitated when he told me, kept saying how stupid of him, putting you in all that danger without it. Something about needing it for next time. Not sure what it is though; looks like a bit of old rubbish to me.' And with that he tossed a crumpled piece of yellowing paper towards Tom before hastily disappearing.

Tom was intrigued. He carefully smoothed out the paper and set it down on the coffee table in front of him. Along one side was a jagged edge, as if it had been ripped hurriedly out of the book it belonged to. The paper seemed ancient – it was fragile and brittle, but apart from one or two spots of mould here and there it was blank. It dawned on him that perhaps he should turn it over. As he did so he gasped with surprise. Staring back at him was a map. 'The Cathedral,' he whispered, his breath quickening – 'it's the Cathedral.'

In the bottom right hand corner three names had been hurriedly scribbled in ink. Tom read them out loud: 'Nathaniel Rowbottom, Osberto Reynolds and Obadiah Barebones.' A broad smile broke across his face. He continued reading what was written underneath the names: 'The Map of 12 – a map for your mission.'

There was something else too. He had noticed a particularly stubborn piece of wax encrusted on the map. He picked away at it and attempted to read aloud what was underneath as some of the writing became legible:

'Jack Postwick, the rhyming Clock-Jack...found here in the South Transept...and also' ...Tom picked away furiously at the wax... 'his brother Jim.' He broke out into a cold sweat, his heart pounding. 'I don't believe it,' he said incredulously, 'it was Jack who had the brother – he never said!' The writing continued, but was faint and difficult to read. 'Jim, the second Clock-Jack – lost to us and imprisoned...'

There were more words but they were impossible to read.

'Emma!' he yelled, his breathing becoming ever faster. 'Emma, come quickly.' He heard her bedroom door open and the sound of footsteps hurrying down the stairs. He opened his mouth to shout once more, but the words stuck in his throat. The map was beginning to change. As it lay there in front of him it lost its spots of mould and its crumpled look, transforming before his very eyes. In no time at all it became as crisp and clear as the day it was made. It became obvious that it was not just the Cathedral that had been drawn upon it. A whole host of other buildings, plans, diagrams and accompanying notes gradually emerged. The Map of 12 took form and was revealed. The Norman Castle, market place and French borough were all clearly drawn. Countless medieval churches, the Great Hospital, and Guildhall all jostled for position and were crammed in next to underground passageways and labyrinthine tunnels, all connected with countless arrows pointing this way and that. Tom noticed a carefully drawn fiery dragon indicating the location of Dragon Hall – the great trading hall on the river Wensum. It appeared that the three previous time travellers had sketched all this in a vain attempt to locate the whereabouts of the imprisoned second Clock-Jack. He was held somewhere within this vast City. Tom was speechless as he tried to take it all in.

And then the final words took shape and formed right there in front of him...

Jim, the second clockjack, lost to us and imprisoned by those who oppose the City of Light.

Jim must be rescued

The last part of the sentence took an agonising few seconds more to reveal itself.

...by you, Tom!

He gasped and looked up as Emma came into the room.

About us

Saul Penfold is an educationalist and writer, producing books, trails and learning materials for a range of heritage sites. He has been a teacher and the Head of Education at Norwich Cathedral. 'The 3 Serpents of the North Door' is his first book for children. He lives in North Norfolk with his wife and two children and spends much of his time drinking tea. He enjoys music, art, cinema and the sea.

To discuss 'The 3 Serpents of the North Door' and his forthcoming books in the 'City of Light' series, contact Saul on saul@serpentbooks.co.uk or visit www.serpentbooks.co.uk

Jim Kavanagh is an artist and illustrator with a background in graphic design. His work has ranged from children's books to magazines and advertising. He's even done rather scary things like draw at special events in front of huge crowds of people. Occasionally he exhibits landscapes, nudes and other proper arty stuff in galleries. He has also been known to write and act in plays, involving false moustaches and silly costumes. Living in Norwich has given him a keen interest in the City's history and a happy association with Norwich Cathedral, as a guide and also drinking lots of tea in the Refectory.

Emma Bridgewater lives in North Norfolk with her husband Matthew Rice and their four children. She started a design company in 1985, which has grown to incorporate a factory in Stoke on Trent, shops in Edinburgh and London plus a thriving on-line business (www.emmabridgewater.co.uk). Her cosy homewares are familiar to many households. She is a lay-canon of Norwich Cathedral and she firmly believes that we should all visit our churches and cathedrals much more often, whether to pray, think, sight-see or even just to get out of the rain.

Norwich Cathedral is a place of great beauty, worship and history. It offers a year round programme of events, activities and exhibitions for people of all ages. To find out more visit www.cathedral.org.uk or telephone 01603 218320. Norwich Cathedral is part of Norwich 12.

Norwich 12 is the UK's finest collection of individually outstanding heritage buildings spanning the Norman, medieval, Georgian, Victorian and modern eras. Charting an extraordinary journey through the history of one of England's great cities, Norwich 12 offers a unique visitor experience which embraces the legacy of these iconic buildings, the pivotal roles they continue to play today and the remarkable cityscape which weaves them together. 'The 3 Serpents of the North Door' has been made possible thanks to funding from the Treasury's 'Invest to Save' Budget, which was secured for Norwich 12 by Norwich Heritage Economic and Regeneration Trust (HEART), the charity set up to act as an umbrella organisation for all the heritage on offer in the City.